SPIRE

A. CUTHBERTSON

THE BIZARCHIVES

The Bizarchives
Weird Tales of Monsters, Magic, and Machines

Presented by
The Midgard Institute
of Science Fiction & Fantasy Literature

Copyright © 2022 by A. Cuthbertson and The Bizarchives

All rights reserved.

No part of this book may be reproduced in any form or by any electronic or mechanical means, including information storage and retrieval systems, without written permission from the author, except for the use of brief quotations in a book review.

CONTENTS

Part I 1

Part II 43

PART ONE

Thaig grabbed a pickaxe from one of the miners and swung it hard at the patch of iridescent material at the end of the shaft. With a strange *clinking* noise, a chunk of the material crumbled. Glittering fragments lay all over the hewn floor of the shaft, catching the light from the lantern-strips on the ceiling. The fragments were mostly milky-white, with pearlescent hues expressing themselves differently depending on the angle at which Thaig looked at them.

He looked at the hole that he had made in the shining patch of the wall. He dug the end of the pickaxe in and scratched and scraped, enlarging the hole. There was nothing but more of the same strange material; milky-white, mysterious, shades shifting over its surface.

He squatted down, mystified, chewing his lip. Thaig was too tall for the low tunnel dug into the rock here; he was supervising this operation now, and even though his mining crew were all big and burly, Thaig was considerably larger than any of them. He had thought that his digging days were far behind him, but he was happy to find that he could still swing a pickaxe harder than anyone. He had spent most of the last few months behind a console since being promoted to exploration geologist, but he still kept himself very fit.

He rested the pickaxe against the wall and grabbed a fragment of the shiny material. He rubbed it back and forth between his thumb and forefinger, holding it up to the light. He pressed it; it was hard, but he felt like the material was ever-so-slightly yielding to his press, as though it was malleable and chalky. He pocketed it and stood up.

"Well," he announced to the men behind him, "that's a new one. Never seen anything like it." He had rushed down here as soon as he had heard the reports relayed over the miner's comms, up to his office on the surface.

His office, and the entrance to this mine, Mine 9, were five miles out from the centre of the last city on this barren, calamity-stricken planet: the city called Spire.

Spire was a miserable jumble of pre-fabricated buildings huddled around a gigantic, mile-high spiked protrusion which jutted out from the ground, as though this accursed planet was pointing an accusing talon at the heavens above for abandoning it. The black talon was of unknown origin, and had many strange properties which continued to confound those who studied it.

The small planet, now known simply as "IV", had been designated for mining and seeded with colonies by an off-world human population centuries ago. Since then, savage storms, freak geological accidents, eruptions, diseases, civil unrest, and all other manner of ills had befallen the isolated little planet. The only place that seemed safe, and indeed the only thing that seemed to keep them safe, was the ten or so miles around that strange, hypnotising spire which gave the last city on IV its name.

The inhabitants mined. They mined because it was the only thing they knew how to do, it was the only reason they were here. They mined until the off-worlders deemed their operation profitable enough to return to collect them. They mined until the off-worlders decided that the planet was exhausted of all mineable material, and that the miners would be of more use elsewhere. Presumably, they would then be collected and evacuated, transported away to somewhere better.

Many didn't survive that long, as the growing Spire graveyards attested. Thaig's generation, and those younger than him, had all been born here, in Spire. His father had been a miner, of course, and his mother had tended the farms. His memories of them were dim.

Many petitioned to go off-world prematurely, Thaig included. Few petitions were answered, and even fewer were successful. Those that were successful went quickly and quietly. Thaig suspected this was to keep morale high among those that remained.

Thaig rubbed his ginger-stubbled chin, lost in thought while he waited for his subordinates' replies. His wide-set blue eyes were bloodshot. He had become reliant on stimulants to keep him going through these night-shifts; nothing illegal, he didn't want to lose his job, and this mining-colony-turned-settlement had only two punishments for criminals: death, or forced labour: usually mining, deep mining, down where it was hot, dangerous, and often resulted in death anyway.

Whether or not it was illegal to be wired on these things while in charge of dangerous mining operations was a different matter. Thaig thought it better not to bother asking anybody about that.

"Yeah, it sure is pretty," answered the senior miner, an old friend and colleague of Thaig's named Brigg. "What the hell do we do with it, though? We were looking for globalt veins. Instead... this? You sure you read the signals right, chief?"

"I'm sure," Thaig snapped, eager to quell any insubordination. "I'm under strict instructions to report anomalies to Central. Cease all activity along this shaft until further notice. Dig along sub-shaft C instead."

"Ack," spat one of the miners, "its solid down that way, even the machines struggle getting through that. Bloody bedrock it is."

Thaig looked at him and stood up as tall as he could in the cramped tunnel. With absolutely no humour in his voice, he said, "Well, perhaps it's best to get started on that sooner rather than later, then."

The crew moaned and shuffled off back down the corridor to their new task.

"Cheers, boss," Brigg said, and he winked at Thaig.

Brigg was a good man, and Thaig knew he owed him a pint for sending him off on a wild goose-chase down an utterly pointless sub-shaft. The truth was that there would be nothing worth finding in that direction and Thaig knew it, but he wasn't about to let the men clock off early. That would reflect badly on him.

He watched his men retreat down the tunnel, then he stood lost in thought, frowning and fingering the iridescent object in his pocket for a moment. Then he made his way back to the main elevator platform which connected the bottom of Mine 9 to the surface, eager to return to his office.

. . .

Thaig sat at his desk, idly playing with the shiny fragment, examining it under a magnifying glass. It wasn't too interesting when it was kept still, but when he moved it around, the way the light played off the surface... it was hypnotising. The subtle shifts in colours and patterns seemed almost impossibly silky and, somehow, *fluid...*

He had combed back through the signals, ran the analyses at the console again, and felt confident that he'd made the right call. Magnetic permeability and susceptibility measurements had been off the charts. He would have been a fool not to follow a lead like that. Now that he looked closer, he supposed that the results may not *definitely* be indicative of globalt veins, but these little tests were never perfectly accurate, and besides, he thought, it was definitely *something,* wasn't it, definitely *something* worth digging out...

Something worth getting to the bottom of.

He had submitted his report to HQ some minutes ago. Or so he thought. He checked the clock - it was actually two hours ago. Thaig flung the fragment into a desk drawer and slammed it shut. Had he really spent hours staring at that thing, playing with it, lost in a trance...? Surely not, he thought.

Although he should have clocked off by now, he'd been told to stay put, as a stooge from Central was on his way to investigate further. That's what they called the government of this horrible place - Central - and he resented every last man that worked for them; especially the one who oversaw this operation: Mulberry. An absolute bastard of a man with the worst moustache on the planet, Thaig thought.

Thaig had to stand to attention whenever this man visited. Mulberry treated him like an idiot, like filth; in Thaig's eyes, the opposite was true. He hated Central, and thought Mulberry was the idiot. The system Central had imposed upon the increasingly paranoid and apathetic residents of Spire, whereby each man was tracked via implants in their arms, and paid in programmable tokens that could only be spent on certain things at certain times, according to their Central whims... it all stuck in his throat.

The truth was that he didn't enjoy this job at all. He didn't think anybody in Spire *really* enjoyed their jobs; they just did them to keep everything going. To keep themselves alive until they hit that mining quota. Even so, his job as a geologist was better than actually mining. He was getting too old to swing a pickaxe all day; if he got paid the same to sit behind a console and send out bore probes and analyse the resulting signals, then he was happy to stay put. Many of his crew were envious of his position, and he fully understood why. They worked men to the grave here.

Annoyed that his thoughts had strayed once again to the same old political grievances, and doubly annoyed that he was supposed to have finished work and left an hour ago, he stood up.

"Fuck Mulberry," he said aloud, and grabbed his heavy black coat. He'd written a detailed enough report for Central to follow, and the crew were still down there, digging away. Brigg would be able to show them to the anomalous substance, glistening down there in the subterranean passages beneath Spire.

Before he left, he opened the drawer again, and put the little iridescent oddment back in his pocket. He wasn't sure why.

———

Thaig walked through the streets of Spire, hands deep in his coat pockets, collar pulled up high, hood pulled down low. It was raining hard and fast. His footsteps splashed through puddles and the drains were overflowing. Everything in the near distance was wrapped in gloomy fog, while a scathing wind blew in from the surrounding wilderness, driving the rain directly into his eyes despite his best efforts with his collar and his hood.

It was night, and it wouldn't be daylight for quite a few hours. The poor lighting situation on the surface meant that all that was visible, all that there was to head towards, was the occasional bright red or yellow light, with outlines made fuzzy by the rainy haze. There was little activity in this sector; nothing could be heard except rain, rain, rain.

He looked up at the tall, thin spindle which dominated the city's skyline, that unnatural talon which pointed at the cloudy heavens above. It was jet black so it was hard to see in the darkness, but its base was lit up by the lights of the Central structures which were built all around it.

While he stared at it, he felt strange, as he always did, as everybody always did... it was difficult to concentrate, difficult to focus. A mix of emotions hit him; a yearning for freedom, fury at the bonds that kept him trapped here, and a desire to push, to grow, to fly free and escape this horrible rock.

There were those who almost worshipped this thing, hailing it as some sort of mystical saviour. The fact that the small area surrounding it had not been wracked by natural disasters that struck everywhere else, that it rained here plentifully, that the sun shone just the right amount to grow crops without scorching them, that the water was clean, that the people remained relatively calm in spite of the bleak situation they faced... this was all nothing short of miraculous, Thaig had to admit.

And he couldn't deny the emotional responses, the outright thought disturbances, and the fuzzy feelings in the head and body when he stared at it for too long. There was something about it that mere science didn't quite understand yet.

Even so, he was skeptical about it having any kind of mystical properties; he had a very rational and materialistic scientist's outlook on life. More importantly, he was a miserable, cynical bastard. To him, it was just a strange piece of rock, which would probably kill hundreds of people when a mining operation eventually disturbed its foundation and toppled it over.

He hated it, but he wasn't allowed to go near it anyway. The Central district was locked off to commoners like him.

He ground his teeth and looked away, resetting his vision straight ahead of him. Was it looking at that weird needle which caused his jaw to grind like this, or was it the stimulants? He sucked at his teeth and chewed his inner cheek, jaw moving left-to-right, right-to-left. Definitely just the spire, he thought, not the stimulants... he'd been careful enough with his dosages.

He headed towards the rough and ready miner's bars, all found in a maze of makeshift streets and alleyways just outside the large Rimwall. Rimwalls encircled the Spire in concentric rings, separating the different districts from each other. Central hid in the innermost ring, in the tallest buildings, keeping a strict eye on everything else and remaining impenetrable to the common man. He didn't even know *who* exactly was in charge; all he knew was the man directly above himself. *Mulberry.*

He needed a drink. These days, in his scientific and managerial role, he would be welcome in more salubrious establishments, but he needed more stims. They weren't *strictly* illegal, he was assured, but getting a prescription for anything had become a nightmare lately. He guessed that the limited supply of certain commodities, seeded here by the offworlders during the initial colonisation of IV, was running low.

There would have been plenty to go around, and of course, modular factories to produce more from a base stock of ingredients. They would have run for a good while, but not everything had survived the ruin that the rest of the planet had suffered. Generations ago, a desperate pilgrimage away from the smashed cities of the other colonies had made its way here, and they had been unable to bring the full suite of amenities with them.

Central kept a tight control over information, but it wasn't hard to guess some things - during Thaig's many long walks around the concentric circles that made up Spire, he hadn't spied anything that looked like a pharmaceutical factory. No, certain supplies were very limited indeed, and it was better to barter for them directly with some crooked physician than to go through official channels. He knew just the man.

He reached his destination: a scuzzy dive of a bar called, enthusiastically, the Offworld Retreat. There was nothing off-world about it. It was definitely, disappointingly, *here*, on IV, in Spire; entering the Offworld Retreat sadly did *not* mean retreating off-world.

Thaig crouched to fit under the door frame, and pulled down his hood. The sound of the rain was replaced by the clinking of mugs, the scraping of chairs, and the grumble of low conversations; the cold and the wet were replaced by warmth. Smoke hovered in the air; he peered through it. Same drab surroundings, same drab clientele. Some of them made eye contact with him, and quickly looked away. There was no decoration to speak of - no frills. It simply served booze, and it attracted those who liked to drink booze.

Thaig removed his coat and hung it on a hook on the wall. Not everybody would leave such a good quality garment on a coat-hook in such a low quality bar; it would of course be stolen. But not everybody was a six foot seven wild-eyed wall of muscles and foul moods like Thaig. He had his own hook. Nobody else dared use it, even when he wasn't there.

He walked up to the bar and grabbed the mug of frothing beer which was already being poured for him when the barkeep saw him come in. With a grunt towards the barkeep, he took it to a table in the corner. The payment would have already left his account via the chip inserted into his left wrist. He didn't know how much was on there; obviously it was enough, or he'd have felt a hot stinging sensation in the wrist to notify him of the failed transaction. He didn't care how much he had. It was due to reset in a few days anyway.

Payday, he thought to himself glumly. Woohoo.

He brought the mug to his lips and drained half of the beer in a single, deep gulp, tilting his head back. When he brought it back down, a thin man was sitting opposite him at his table, smoking and smiling at him.

"What the-" Thaig jumped in his chair. "Why do you do that, man? Why do you always do that? You come out of nowhere, sneak up on me, quiet as a cat, give me the fright of my life and then offer me a smoke, every bloody time."

The man snorted with crude laughter, and held out his packet of cigarettes. "Can't recall ever offering you a cigarette, Thaig. Didn't think you smoked."

"I wouldn't normally." Thaig took one, lit it using the man's lighter, and took a few drags. The men sat in silence for a few seconds.

"You being cryptic as usual, then, big fella? Well, I can't be bothered with small-talk either - no time to find out why you've chosen to take up smoking, today of all days," said the thin man. He wrapped his narrow lips around his skinny cigarette, took a drag, and exhaled out of the corner of his mouth. "You're late, is what I'm trying to say."

The thin man was called Hubert. Hubert was the dodgy doctor that Thaig had come to see - the man with the prescription pills. His bald, misshapen head was adorned with the wrinkles of concern and stress so familiar to the residents of Spire; his brown eyes full of all the familiar sorrows. He was one of the only people alive who enjoyed - or would even dare to try having - such a familiar rapport with the large, difficult, lumbering Thaig.

"Work stuff. Central keeping me back, that Mulberry guy. You know how it is."

"I know how it is, yeah: blame Central when anything goes wrong!" Hubert laughed.

Thaig looked at him humourlessly.

"You got it, then? I got the stims," said Hubert.

From his pocket, Thaig withdrew the item the doctor was after. While doing so, he brushed the chipped pearly fragment from the mine, which was still there in the same pocket.

He slid the item across the table: a first-aid kit, one of the high-quality off-world ones, some of the original colonial stash. When opened, this thing would expand into a one-stop human repair shop, and help easily save lives with its wide range of self-adhesive bandages, gauzes, liquid compresses, and countless other forgotten medical technologies.

It was practically an ancient artefact, but there were tons of them down in the mines. The colony had been seeded with an abundance of them, and they were seldom used in the mine itself, where everybody was well-trained enough to avoid needing to use them. To an illicit doctor like Hubert, they were like gold dust, but getting one from the mines required managerial access.

Thaig pocketed the packets of stims which were thrust upon him, and went back to idly fondling the fragment in his pocket. He remained silent, lost in thought about its origin, about the consequences of walking out of his office when Mulberry was expecting him to be there. Had he been too hasty, he thought, was he overdoing it with the stimulants? What the *hell* was this fragment in his pocket? He'd never seen anything like it…

Hubert leaned across the table. "What's eating you, Thaig," he said, "even for *you* you're quiet tonight."

Thaig looked at him and chewed his lip. "These tablets you've been giving me," he began slowly, "they're the same ones as usual, right? They're not stronger or anything?"

Hubert shrugged and said, "You get what you're given, my friend. You get what I can sneak out under Central's nose. You wanted uppers, you got uppers."

Thaig simply stared at him. He gripped his beer mug uncharacteristically hard, which Hubert noticed.

The doctor shifted uncomfortably in his seat, finished the rest of his cigarette in one inhalation, stubbed it out and stood up, ready to leave. He nodded at Thaig and said, "Maybe ease up on these ones, OK? Low dosage, but different pills. I can't know how everything's gonna affect you, it's trial and error."

"Mmhm."

"Just... go easy, alright? In general. You look like hell. Have another beer, try to relax."

With that, Hubert turned around and walked out of the bar.

Thaig got another beer and tried to relax.

After a few more beers, and still no further towards relaxation, another man joined Thaig at his table. This time, the man was unexpected, and very, very unwelcome. Thaig looked at the man's glazed expression, his heavily-lidded eyes, and his dopey smile. Thaig looked down to the man's jacket and saw it, right there, right where he knew it would be, fastened to the lapel: the badge of the Antennites.

"Have you heard the good word, brother? Have you looked upon it tonight, our Antenna to heaven?"

Thaig said nothing, fixated on the man's badge. The downward facing curve, representing the surface of the planet, and the black line sticking out from it, representing that horrible black tower that all their lives revolved around. Nothing more, Thaig thought to himself, chewing his lip, nothing more interesting than that. Just: black tower. Spire. That's it, just the tower, that bloody tower, he thought-

He inhaled sharply. His mind was racing. He didn't need to top up on stimulants in the bathroom there, did he, really, but you have to test these things, don't you, he thought, you have to know whether it's good stuff-

"Brother?" The man waved a hand in front of Thaig's eyes. Too close.

Thaig frowned.

"Brother?"

"What? I'm not your brother."

"We're all brothers, under the Antenna. It's alive, don't you see? It's alive... it thinks like us. It thinks our thoughts. Meditate upon it, brother. Sit with us and stare, don't resist the feelings you feel... it transmits our souls out to heaven. Like an antenna... you see? You can be free. Free from all this."

Thaig stared at a point just to the left of the man's head. If he was to punch there, he thought, with his right hand, as hard as he could, this man's head would pop like a ripe melon in its attempt to stop his meteoric fist on its rightful passage.

"You see?" repeated the Antennite.

Thaig hated these Antennites. Idiot cultists, he thought, who spent all of their time staring at the one thing he spent most of his time trying to avoid looking at: the black towering formation at the centre of Spire. It turned their brains into mush. There were hundreds of them now, walking around, clogging up the streets, talking their nonsense... some of them even wore white robes with black lines emblazoned on them.

While the man's words seemed profound, he had

heard a thousand variations on the themes, many of them contradictory.

It was an antenna that transmitted their thoughts out into heaven!

It was an antenna that transmitted signals from the heavens back to them!

Messages from dead relatives, messages from the future, promises of protection, promises of doom - all of it, depending on which one of these freaks you spoke to, and what visions that awful spire had filled their head with that day. He'd heard it all before, and he had no time for it.

For once, he thought, Central should do something useful and lock them all up, and whip it out of them. Get them back to work. But Central was too busy, and resources were too short, to deal with some idiot-cult.

Thaig thought that they were bad for productivity. They abandoned their mining duties to stare at a rock all day instead. The sooner the colonists reached their mining quota, the sooner they were all off this rock - he felt like giving the Antennites a good shake. Did they want to be here forever? They probably did - how else would they be able to stare at their beloved black spire all day?

Caught up in the intensity of his thoughts, and not having perfect control over his jaw, he bit his tongue quite hard. He groaned and winced and sat back, spilling his beer as he shot his arms out in surprise.

"I see you are in pain, brother, and in shock," droned the Antennite, "trying to come to terms with the true nature of our reality. Come with me, and I can help you to understand."

"I've juthst bit my pfthucking tongue!" Thaig cried.

"Ah," the Antennite said in a sympathetic tone, "you are simple of mind. I didn't realise, my child, forgive me. In that case, come with me, I can show you something very *special*..."

Thaig frowned. He had been insulted precisely once in his life, when he was a child, and the teacher that had made that remark wore dentures for the rest of his life.

Everything sped up in a way that Thaig found impossible to control, and before he knew it, he had stood up and lashed out with one tree-trunk arm, and his right fist had shot toward that spot just to the left of the Antennite's head. The cultist and his chair both fell backward in a spray of blood-mist and the man lay there on the floor, motionless.

Disappointingly, but probably for the best, the man's head had not exploded like a melon. But he'd definitely sustained some serious damage. Thaig looked around. Predictably, everybody was staring at him.

"What?"

They returned to their drinks sheepishly.

Thaig stood and looked down at the man he had knocked out. "Freaks," he spat, and stormed out of the bar after grabbing his coat.

———

Thaig arrived back at his apartment. He stood out on the tenement balcony, waving his left wrist over the lockpad again and again, thoroughly soaked from the incessant rain. Ironic, he thought, that his position had enabled him to upgrade to a better apartment, one higher up in the building, with a view... and an entrance on an *outdoor* balcony.

His old apartment was in a corridor downstairs. Indoors. If he was having lockpad problems in the wee hours of the morning ten years ago, at least he'd be dry.

He lived in a decent residential neighbourhood, close to the centre, in an old residential module containing about fifty dwellings. It had been packed up and brought here by convoy from one of the old cities down towards the equator of IV. He had forgotten its name. He had forgotten what happened there, too - earthquake, was it? Scorching heatwave? Whatever. The housing module was here now. In Spire. And he couldn't get inside the blasted thing.

"Bastard," he said aloud, while rainwater dripped down his nose and into his mouth. He waved his wrist over the lockpad again, pressed his wrist up against it, bashed it against it repeatedly, all to no avail. He grumbled and looked for something to put through the window. He needed to get to bed, by any means necessary.

Suddenly, without his wrist being near the door, it slid open. Shaking his head, he walked into his sitting room and took off his coat. Bloody ancient technology, he thought, what use was it being tracked the whole time with these damn wrist implants if they weren't even any *good?* They had all of the downsides with none of the benefits. He'd have to get that lockpad looked at too, it was obviously faulty-

He paused. Something was off. He could smell something: sweat, cigarette smoke. Not his own. He kept his apartment clean. Untidy, sure, but it was clean. Dishes and cups lay piled up in heaps, but they were sparkling fresh. He washed his clothes regularly. He didn't usually smoke, so why could he smell it so strongly? He wasn't some dirty addict or anything like that. He chewed his lip and his jaw slid from left-to-right, right-to-left. Slowly, warily, he turned around.

Surely enough, two very serious looking Central goons had padded stealthily into the sitting room from the corridor. They wore the drab grey uniforms of the security services, with badges on their chests. Plain black bar, vertical. Representing - Thaig gritted his teeth - that damned spire.

He motioned towards his plastic-leather sofa. He barely sat on the thing; it was in pristine condition, much like most of his furniture. There was a coffee table in front of it with nothing on it except a crumpled empty packet of Hubert's stimulants. He used this apartment to sleep, wash, and eat breakfast, and then he spent the rest of his time at Mine 9 or the Offworld Retreat. The whole apartment, much like the bar he liked to frequent, was sparsely decorated.

He had a picture on the windowsill, his sole concession to sentimentality; a picture of his parents at their wedding, framed by both sets of grandparents. They were smiling happy smiles; looking at it made him happy, too. He wondered whether he'd ever have such a happy day. He had all but given up on finding a wife - not too many women frequented the Offworld Retreat. They certainly didn't frequent Mine 9. A lot of the best women married into Central. He couldn't blame them - they did what was best for themselves, just like he did.

"Take a seat, gents," Thaig said uneasily.

"We'd prefer to stand," one of them said. He walked forward and stood on the far side of Thaig's coffee table.

"Me too. Care for a drink?" Thaig motioned towards the kitchenette where a small kettle and some jars of powdered coffee and teas were sitting on the bench.

"No."

"Ah," Thaig said, "well, if it's not thirst that brings you into my home uninvited, what the hell is it?"

There was an awkward moment or two of silence. The other man cleared his throat. "You were supposed to be at your office, Thaig."

Thaig laughed, for the first time in a long time. "Is *that* what this is about? What a waste of time! You can read the reports! What need is there to ambush me in my home for that? *Really* keen to crack down on any kind of insubordination, are you? This is tyrannical," he spat, "inhuman. Right. I've learned my lesson. You've told me off. Now get out!"

They moved slowly across up the living room towards him, one on either side. Thaig stepped back warily.

"If you're quite finished," said one, "we need you to come with us. Just stand still there for a moment."

"You can't arrest me for this," Thaig spluttered, "I've done nothing wrong! I was sick of waiting, that's all!"

"All the same," the other man said "we just need you to come with us. Don't make this difficult, Thaig."

"You can't! Tell that bastard Mulberry that he's overstepped the line this time!" He was conscious of the little pearly fragment in his pocket,; for some reason he wanted to protect it and hide it from the two men in grey.

The Central enforcers stopped, holding their hands up to their ears, obviously listening to their comms earpieces.

"Is that so?" said one.

"Sounds like you've been in a bar fight, Thaig," said the other. "Now you *are* under arrest."

"No... wait, you didn't know that before you came here? What were you *really* here for?" Thaig was ultra-paranoid now, wide-eyed, eyes darting left to right. He subtly adopted a fighting stance, slightly to one side, left shoulder forward, right fist balled up.

"Stand down, Thaig. Stand still while we handcuff you."

"You can't arrest me for leaving my office!"

"We can arrest you for nearly killing a man in a bar."

"Ah, well that you technically *can* arrest me for," Thaig conceded.

"We know. Now, turn around and hold your hands behind your back."

"...No."

At this, the Central goons both lost their patience. Crowding Thaig back towards his front door, they lunged for him. Deceptively quick on his feet, possibly owing to those prescription stimulants, Thaig dodged between them and kicked over his coffee table before turning around. With more space in the room now, he had a more even playing field.

He knew this would likely mean a forced labour sentence, but he wasn't thinking straight, and he wasn't about to just go down for *nothing* without a fight, everything was going too fast again, what were they playing at, he thought, sending two enforcers into his house like this-

He looked down and gasped.

One of the men who had just lunged at him held a dagger. Not a standard shock-baton, but a very sharp and nasty-looking military-grade knife. Without a moment to think on it more, the men pressed the assault again.

Thaig was big, strong, and quick, but had no combat training like these two. He'd have to rely on his wits... and perhaps superior knowledge of his apartment. He grabbed a floor-standing lamp and threw it at them. It did nothing, but the men were wary, on the back foot, confused, expecting some kind of trap or hidden weapon.

There was none, but Thaig followed up like a hurricane. He smashed his fist into the face of the man carrying the knife, with his whole weight behind it. The man crumpled instantly, unconscious.

The other man lunged at him now, having produced one of the same knives. Thaig dodged easily, and managed to trip him up by kicking over his waste-bin into the man's path as he passed. In a desperate attempt to prevent his own murder, Thaig was upon the man, raining blows upon his head, and he didn't stop until his fingers and knuckles were bloody and raw.

Thaig gasped for breath. The man's head was pulped. He'd killed him. He'd never killed a man before... a Central enforcer, no less. He was in big trouble.

But - he reminded himself - they'd tried to kill him first. He'd been in the worst kind of trouble already, before he had even made it home - this was nothing less than an assassination attempt. They had tried to make him believe he was under arrest, tried to get him to turn around - and what would he have gotten then, for obeying the authorities? A knife in the back, that's what.

What the hell was going on? What was Central up to, he thought, and why him?

He walked over to the unconscious man. He stooped down and pulled out the man's comms earpiece, and inserted it into his own ear.

"Come in," he heard, "come in. Jhed is dead, showing no pulse from his implant. Yours is still active. Is the target neutralised? Confirm."

Thaig held up the man's wrist, where his implant mic would be, and in the best possible rendition of the man's voice that he could muster, said, "confirmed."

"Good," came a relieved voice. "Report to Mine 9 immediately. Situation under control here, too. All targets neutralised."

Thaig's heart sank. Neutralised? Brigg? All his boys?

He'd report to Mine 9 alright. He'd tear through the place like a bore through rock.

"Oh, and Kreg?" The voice in the earpiece continued,

"Thaig's still alive. We're tracing his implant - still showing a pulse. You haven't been as thorough as you thought you were. Slit his throat and get to Mine 9. Clean-up crew will be there in an hour. Over and out."

Thaig looked down at his wrist. He looked at one of the knives that had been dropped on the floor. This was going to be grim. He reached for his stimulants and swallowed two at once. The implant had to go, or they'd know his vitals and his exact whereabouts at all times.

He picked up the knife and dangled it over his left arm, where he knew the implant was. In his left hand, he gripped the glimmering fragment from the mine shaft tightly. Whether it was this that gave him comfort and confidence, or the double-dose of fast-acting stims, he didn't know. With an uncharacteristically cool head, he gritted his teeth, and began to cut.

———

Thaig kept to the shadows. He wore ill-fitting security garb that he had stripped from one of his assailants. He was under no illusions, though; anybody who'd been briefed to look for a massive, bleeding, wild-eyed ginger nutcase would have spotted him easily. He was thankful that there were still very few people on the streets, that it was still rainy and foggy, and that it was still dark.

He'd almost made it back to Mine 9, and he didn't have long before daybreak would make it impossible for him to get there undetected. He winced with every step. His arm was heavily bandaged; he was sore and he was implantless. He was effectively dead. He couldn't buy anything, couldn't get through doors, couldn't receive money or benefits…. couldn't be tracked.

It had seemed extreme at first, but Thaig was already a dead man in the eyes of Central. They'd tried to kill him, after all. His implant hadn't worked on the doorpad by the time he got home; he realised, with a chill, that Central had probably ceased all of its functions except the location and pulse tracking by then. It was the agents who had *let him in* to his own apartment.

He shook his head. The sheer gall of it.

He had extracted the living goon's implant, too. After the brutal self-surgery he had just performed, it had seemed pleasant by comparison. He had slit the man's throat beforehand. His second kill had shocked him far less than his first. He felt numb, and more than a little unhinged.

He'd studied the implants in his idle hours at work, at the console when he was supposed to be analysing bores. Hubert had lent him a textbook and had explained things in great detail over a few beers in the Offworld Retreat.

He tossed away the parts of the man's implant which controlled sensors, trackers and the like, and carefully withdrew the thin, flat disc which activated doorpads. With any luck, the death of the Central goon wouldn't have automatically disabled the security access programmed into the disc; he should be able to breeze into Mine 9 with this.

And if he couldn't, well, he'd just maul as many people as he could until they took him down.

They'd tried to kill him, and they had apparently neutralised his boys down in the mine already; he wanted blood. He felt a duty of care towards them. Indeed, if any of them were showing signs of exhaustion or distress, it was his job as supervisor to get them out of there, and he'd done that plenty of times. And he'd certainly pulled them out of some dangerous situations before; avoiding gas build-ups, cave-ins, and perilous openings and drops. He'd never lost a man yet.

And Central had just waltzed through and killed them all? He wanted to kill *them* all. He wanted to burn Central to the ground.

There was more than just revenge on his mind, though. There was still the burning question: *why?* Why had all this come about so shortly after finding - he gasped as things began to fall into place - after finding that strange little vein of pearlescent material? He still carried the beautiful fragment with him, the one that he'd pocketed in the mine shaft - what was it? Why had it caused a spate of murders - by the government, no less?

He considered the fragment to be one of his only treasured possessions, now. His second sentimentality, after the picture of his parents, which he'd folded up and pocketed before leaving. He'd made sure to keep hold of the fragment - he felt an odd attachment to it now. Gripping it while going through the pain of cutting out his implant had, bizarrely, helped him through it.

As the white-hot pain had seared through him, as he'd yelped and squealed, he'd gripped harder, and he'd sustained visual disturbances. The room around him had become white, milky, and pearlescent... he'd seen the fragment, raw and bleeding. A confusing mix of imagery,but, nevertheless, one which had helped to take his mind off the pain. Furthermore, he'd felt oddly bolstered, as though it were spurring him on.

He knew that he was really pushing himself psychologically with these acts. All of this, while being high on stims and hunted by the law. But if the only mental disturbance he'd have was pretty pearlescent imagery and that breezy feeling of bravery... well, he was alright with that. He felt oddly calm, like he was acting in accordance with some higher purpose, as though he was doing the *right thing*.

He was going to kill people this morning. Probably quite a few of them.

The "clean-up crew" that Central comms had promised would find nothing but ashes. He'd left his stove on, with a bunch of fabric strewn on top of it and shoved into the main oven. It would be blazing away merrily by now. The modules had fire-retardant walls and floors; he wouldn't have put any of the other residents in danger. He wasn't an *indiscriminate* murderer, like the scum who worked for Central security, and he felt like that was an important distinction to make to himself.

The flesh and bones of his assailants would be steadily blackening, though, and he smiled at the thought. Worthless Central goons, he thought. Assassins for hire. He whistled a tune as he walked, and popped another stimulant pill out of its blister. What the hell, he thought; it wouldn't hurt to have a little boost for what he was about to do, would it?

Thaig slipped into the Mine 9 complex undetected. There was nobody up here, thankfully, no Central scum. He supposed that they would all be down below, treading on the corpses of his colleagues. Above ground, there wasn't much that interested him on the best of days, just ore transportation belts to the refinery modules, cranes, and other machinery. This time, though, it was too quiet. None of the usual vehicles went in and out, none of the machinery was running. The lights were dimmer than normal.

He stuck close to the fence, avoiding the spotlights, and walked up to the drab building which contained his office. Part of him wanted to go straight down the elevator to try to save his friends, but he remembered the cold report given in the comms earpiece at his apartment: *neutralised*. He would be too late.

No, he decided, he wanted to gain access to his office and have a look at the cameras that showed the situation down in the shafts. He also hoped that he would be able to enact some kind of revenge from up there; maybe drive a bore probe or two through his team's murderers. He chewed his lips as he envisioned the potential carnage.

He walked up to his office and held up Kreg's door-pad-disc to the pad. *Bingo*, he thought, as the door slid open. For some reason, he'd been confident that this would work - Central were obsessed with control, but they weren't very competent when it came down to it. They'd clearly be able to tell that Kreg was dead if they checked his vitals, but his access hadn't been revoked yet.

Amateurs, Thaig thought. He snorted. A great deal of Central's control over them was just the *illusion* of control, the illusion of smooth, competent omnipotence. They simply weren't good enough to execute it. The technology was good, but it wasn't *that* good. There was still plenty of room for human error, and plenty of room to exploit those errors.

He checked behind the door for hidden assailants then he looked around the rest of the room. There were none - the light came on above his head automatically as he walked in. Movement sensors, he thought. Cheap bastards. Primitive tech. He was never sure whether they were activated from his implant or just by the movement of his body - now he knew.

He saw that his desk had been ransacked. They'd taken everything, and his desk drawers hung open, skewed sadly aflop. He walked over to them - they were empty. He didn't keep much in there, but he had stashed one of those medical kits in the bottom one to trade for stims later. It was gone. They probably knew he was a thief now, too, but that was the least of his worries.

His computer terminal was still on; good, he thought. He leaned over the desk and tapped some keys. Everything sprang to life and the light made him squint his bloodshot eyes. Odd - he'd turned it off before he left. They'd obviously turned his computer on while they stripped his office. They were likely stripping that, too, deleting files... removing all trace of him, he realised bitterly. Preparing for his replacement.

It felt so strange to lose everything in the space of one evening, to become a dead man walking like this. He felt hollow.

He checked the cameras that looked down into the mine. He saw, as he'd suspected, a pile of corpses heaped up on the main elevator. He couldn't make out individual details, but he knew that it was his men. He knew that they were dead before he saw them, but it still hurt him to see it. He bit his lip angrily. Looking at the other cameras, he could see men in full body-suits with helmets and visors, the likes of which he had never seen, moving in and out of the shaft that contained the glittering vein.

What were they *doing*, he thought to himself, what was so important that they had gone to all this trouble...?

He checked the messaging function on the terminal - all logs deleted. All records of everything found in Mine 9, deleted. He couldn't believe it. Like nothing they ever found here was worth anything... their life's work, gone. They *had* found a bunch of good material over the years, and made a sizeable contribution towards the colony's mining quotas... all deleted? What sense did that make?

He checked the Sent Messages function and - he shook his head again - he saw that they had neglected to purge these. *Amateurs,* he repeated to himself. He could see one sent just a couple of hours ago. He frowned - that couldn't have been sent by him - some Central goon must have sent a message to their bosses from this terminal.

He opened it, half in excited glee, and half in disbelief

of their sheer arrogance and negligence. They really didn't think much of the common worker, did they? The message had been sent to a random string of letters and numbers that must have been some kind of Central security foil, something memorised but impossible to guess. It read:

> *Thaig not present at office upon arrival. He was always difficult, but this is an uncharacteristic level of disobedience. Suspected depression or burnout - confirmed to be stealing. His erratic behaviour marks him as being particularly dangerous. Trackers show him to be at a bar called the Offworld Retreat, in close proximity to Suspect Practitioner H. Location too public for neutralisation. His behaviour patterns are predictable enough to suggest that he will head home after three hours of drinking, where he will be alone. Agents dispatched to his apartment.*
>
> *All other targets neutralised. Clean-up crew activated.*

Thaig cursed under his breath. It was so cold, so callous of them to talk about murder like this. His *own* murder. And were his habits really that predictable? What Central knew about him, or could find out about him at the click of a button, made him turn his nose up in disgust. At least they didn't know about the stimulants, yet... that was between him and Hubert, but it looked like Hubert might be in some danger too.

He scrolled down further, there was more:

Root neutralised. Concerning to find one this far out. We thought we had better control over this. We thought we had it surrounded. We haven't had to close a mine in three years, and the last one was only two miles away from the centre. This one is five miles away. First time we've caught one this far away - this root must snake underneath and around. Must redouble pacification attempts.

Remaining at Mine 9 until clean-up complete.
-Cent. Mulberry

Central Mulberry... what a bastard, Thaig thought. How glad he was that he hadn't waited around to meet him last night. He'd have gotten a dagger through the ribs with no prior warning. He'd have been a sitting duck. He was *very* glad that he'd had that sudden flash of insubordination. But, to have it last night of all nights, when he was just about to be murdered... very strange. While he mulled this over, he rolled the shining fragment around in his palm.

He had a flash of realisation - a closed mine, three years ago, two miles out from Central - that was Mine 6!

They'd told everybody that it was a horrible cave in, a tragic loss of life due to carelessness on the overseer's part. They'd hauled him off and given him the death penalty for negligence...

Or, he now realised, they'd murdered everybody for finding one of these "roots" below ground. With special attention paid to the man in his own role, the overseer, the Exploration Geologist. Well, he'd give them their comeuppance. He'd teach them for crying wolf. Thaig *was* the wolf. Slowly, deliberately, he used the terminal to prime and then aim Mine 9's contingent of six-foot wide bore probes. All of them.

He had his mind on another little surprise for them, too. They used more than just bores to clear areas of rock down there. He could see from the cameras that there must be twenty Central goons down in the central shaft... he hoped Mulberry was among them.

His mind raced as he set up the bores. He chewed his lips until he tasted blood; his heart thumped. What was this conspiracy that he was uncovering? He'd come here for a rampage, for satisfaction, for closure... and he'd just found more questions. More itches to scratch. So they called that glittering pearlescent vein of material down in the shafts a "root", eh... was it from a plant? A tree? Was that just their term for it - was it just the root of a larger vein of rocky white material, miles away?

He primed his other surprises, which were all contained in secure crates down at the bottom of the surface-elevator. They couldn't be primed from anywhere else but this exact terminal. There were more of them stashed throughout Mine 9, in various tunnels and checkpoints.

They'd have heard the beeping down there, for sure.

He saw some people on the cameras inspecting the crates, watched them getting anxious. They had about three minutes. With a vindictive smile on his face, he switched on the loading-mode on the surface elevator. As a safety measure - he cackled at the irony - as a *safety measure*, it was now utterly deactivated for *five* minutes.

He popped a stimulant to celebrate his victory. He watched them down there on the cameras, running around, frantically pressing buttons, fleeing down tunnels and trying to climb the walls. They wouldn't get anywhere. He looked to the pile of corpses, his dead friends. This was for them. He pushed a button and released the bore-probes. Down below, gigantic probes thrust themselves through rock - and empty space - in all directions, all around Mine 9.

He saw a rumble, and then the cameras cut out.

He stood up and stretched. Two and a half minutes until the grand finale. This was going to cause a *lot* of chaos. Maybe even enough chaos to provide a distraction that would allow him to slip into Central. He had to try, at least. The ground beneath him began to shake and wobble - and it wasn't the near-lethal quantity of drugs coursing through his veins which made it appear to do so. It really *was* shaking as the bores did their thing.

He heard footsteps outside and froze - somebody was running up the metal stairs outside. He looked around -

there was nowhere to hide. He dropped low and adopted a rangy stance, ready for whoever came through the door.

And there he was, in a silly little grey cap denoting his status: *Mulberry*. What a bastard, Thaig thought, what an absolute bastard. He looked at the man's pompous face and frowned. Mulberry had a large nose and a small chin; high, thin cheekbones; and small, squinting eyes. Thaig focused intently on his horrible wispy little moustache.

He disliked this man intensely, and now that their differences in status didn't matter, he was going to do something about it.

Mulberry gasped when he saw him. "Thaig! You shouldn't be here!"

"Sorry to disappoint," growled Thaig. He lunged at Mulberry.

Mulberry pulled a black object up from his belt. Thaig stopped in his tracks. He couldn't believe what he saw; he'd only ever read about them or heard talk of them in hushed whispers: a *gun*. He knew what they did and how dangerous they were. They were strictly forbidden on mining colonies. This thing must have been one of a few smuggled here by overseers of the original IV colony project, centuries ago.

Mulberry looked to Thaig's bandaged arm, his dishevelled appearance, his ill-fitting stolen grey security uniform. Finally, he looked him in the eyes.

"My word," said Mulberry, "you look like a wild animal!"

"You look like a wimp hiding behind a gun," Thaig riposted.

"Hah!" laughed Mulberry. "Tell me - what did you do, messing with the controls there? I've lost contact to the men below. What's that rumbling?"

"Bores." Thaig smiled a placid, happy smile.

"Ah, think you're clever, do you? Killed a few of my men? Well, you'll pay for that. Tell me how to stop those bores, or I'll shoot you."

Thaig laughed at him.

Mulberry paced around the room, gun continuously pointed at Thaig. "We knew you were on the loose. We'd assumed you'd gone into hiding. That would have been the smart thing to do, Thaig. You weren't exactly very subtle... two agents, dead in an inferno. And no remains of a big, dumb idiot to be found anywhere?"

He walked to the terminal, gun still aimed at Thaig.

Thaig said nothing.

Mulberry continued, "We didn't think even *you* would be stupid enough to come here, though. This really is the last place you should have come. Now, tell me how to stop the bores. You could still save lives, Thaig. Be a hero."

"Even if I could save them, I wouldn't."

"You don't know anything, Thaig," shouted Mulberry, "you'll doom us all. You've no idea how deep this goes, you've no idea what happens to people who come across those..."

"Roots?" Thaig finished his sentence.

Mulberry looked away from the terminal and frowned at Thaig. "How... ah, you've seen a report."

"What are they, those roots? What makes them worth

all of this secrecy and murder? They were good men, we were a good team... I'm a good man, damn it!" Thaig shouted.

Mulberry locked eyes with him and gritted his teeth. "Thaig, I'll only make this offer once. We'll take you under our wing, tell you everything... but you have to call off these bores. You have to save my men."

"I know the feeling, Mulberry, you bastard! Now you'll know the feeling of having *your* men die in a hole, while you're miles away on the surface, helpless!"

"Please, Thaig! No more death!"

"I told you, there's no saving them. It's done. Mine 9 is done."

"Nonsense," said Mulberry, "the entire mine will *not* collapse due to a few rogue bores, but many of the men trapped inside will die pointlessly. Disable them immediately!"

Grinning, Thaig counted down in his head. Ten, nine, eight... he'd been counting down the seconds from when he set the timers on his surprises.

Mulberry began to sense that something was wrong. "What the hell is this, Thaig? I mean it, I'll shoot!"

"Five, four..." he said out loud.

"THAIG!"

"Three, two, one-"

An earthquake shook beneath their feet. Down in the mine below, hundreds of tons of mining-grade explosives exploded all at once. Mulberry fell over and shot the gun by accident - it hit the terminal which went up in a cascade of sparks.

The room shook; the ground shook; there were cracking and snapping noises everywhere, metal whined and groaned, large structures and machines fell to the floor with a series of loud bangs. The ground slid beneath their feet, the entire office building juddered and the contents of the room flew into the air.

Thaig dived on Mulberry, grabbed his gun, and thumped his head with the butt for good measure. Mulberry struggled and fought back like a cornered cat, blood pouring from his nose into his eyes. Thaig was about to turn the gun around and shoot him, until an almighty squeal and a shift in the floor beneath them threw him off Mulberry and away towards the door.

Thaig's explosive surprises had caused a total mine collapse, a structural catastrophe. He had brought the earthquakes that the horrible black spire supposedly kept away; he had overcome his arch-nemesis at the centre of Central and caused massive damage to the city of Spire. He didn't care - for him, all that mattered now was the truth. Justice. *Freedom*.

His whole office block was sliding down into a massive hole that was quickly spreading from the elevator shaft. The quaking sides of the shaft had dislodged the covering, and it had tumbled down into the hole, leaving the shaft completely open to the sky and the incessant rain. Before he climbed out of the door, which was now above him, he took aim at Mulberry and fired.

Unused to the recoil, he missed miserably. The bullet lodged in his desk, which Mulberry was leaning on, trying to stand up; their eyes met for a moment and a look of mutual pure hatred passed between them.

Feeling that this was his last chance to escape, Thaig pulled himself out through the door. He emerged into utter chaos; loud sirens from all directions, shouts, screams, and the light of dawn breaking through the clouds. He watched, fascinated, as a crane slid down into the growing hole, knocking another one over on its way past, causing a domino-effect as it in turn crashed into more buildings and fences and mining equipment. The noise was deafening.

He dropped down and jogged away, into the oncoming crowd of emergency services and concerned citizens who were running towards the scene, hoping to melt into the crowd and make his way to Central. Given the level of chaos he'd caused, that shouldn't be difficult.

Looming above them all, the black spire reached for the heavens, fully visible now in the daylight. It felt like a dagger cutting directly through Thaig's vision, through his skull and his brain, and it bothered him more than ever; he couldn't concentrate on anything unless he made the conscious effort not to look at it. He felt a writhing desire for freedom like never before, a desire to push on towards the end goal, whatever that may be. He didn't know the truth yet, but he was convinced it lay in the Central district, at the bottom of that black column.

He left Mulberry, that absolute *bastard,* to what he hoped was a nightmarish fall to his death at the bottom of Mine 9.

PART TWO

Mayhem raged across Spire. The security forces of Central had lost their tight grip on the city. Burning, looting, and violent assaults ripped through the streets. Sirens and alarms blared everywhere. Rather than one or two grey-suited enforcers being able to cow entire groups of men into submission, they were backed into alleyways in whole squadrons, desperately defending themselves as rioters threw heavy objects at them.

The rain kept pounding down. People slipped over and were set upon by the opposing faction; security versus citizen. Nobody who hit the floor got back up. Mass brawls had erupted, and the rioters seemed to be getting the upper hand. Thaig hoped that they could follow through. Central had all the equipment, all the supply chains, the food, the energy... but the citizens had the *spirit*.

The rioters hadn't bothered to wear masks, Thaig noted; they'd all be tracked through their implants anyway. It seemed that he'd provoked a full-scale uprising. He supposed that a population under such heavy paranoiac stress, mistreated for generations by an overbearing elite, were only ever one major crisis away from bursting at the seams. The people screamed for freedom, whatever that may mean to them; freedom through fire and blood.

Events like this - mine collapses, explosions, pandemics, food shortages - had all happened before, causing minor unrest. But this time was different. It was like a spark had been lit, like a fuse attached to a powderkeg had been set aflame. He fiddled with the shining, sparkling fragment from the mine in his pocket as he wondered what was different this time... something about this felt supernatural.

The chain of events was too unlikely, too fresh in his mind; his ardently materialistic outlook was starting to fray at the edges. Something about the uncovering of this material had set Spire abuzz with energy, but what? *How?* Thaig ruminated over this as he chewed his lip and ground his jaw, taking long, purposeful strides towards the Central buildings that clustered around the base of the black tower.

He'd made his way past the residential districts; the Rimwalls that guarded the successive concentric districts were completely unguarded. Normally people were only able to get through the gates which had specific access to; in a crisis, the gates would either be locked down to everybody or disabled entirely in order to let emergency vehicles through.

Fortunately, this time they were open. The occasional mining rescue truck or fire engine belted through them at speed, along with throngs of thuggish rioters heading in both directions. Whether the vehicles were driven by security forces, or hijacked by joyriders, Thaig didn't have time to ascertain. One nearly ran him over, and he cursed, fighting the urge to turn around and shoot at it with Mulberry's gun.

He'd discarded his security outfit soon after realising that the population had turned on Central; it wasn't the safe disguise it had been a few hours ago. He wore the plain clothes of a commoner, which he had looted from a store near the mining district. Its windows had been smashed through - he had just walked right in and out through the front window. He wore a hat to disguise his fiery red hair, and had his collar pulled up around his neck, attempting to hide his dead-giveaway ginger stubble.

He felt well disguised, but his size still made him stick out. From a distance, he would be alright, but when he got to Central, things might be different. He was prepared for that. The gun weighed heavily in his breast pocket. Hopefully, he thought, he'd only have to use it on Central staff, but anything could happen during a riot.

He felt *good*. He was absolutely full of stimulants. He couldn't remember the last time he'd blinked, and he sure as hell didn't feel like blinking now as he jogged toward the gigantic black column at the centre of the city. He found it increasingly hard to tear his eyes away from it. He was aware of his surroundings, almost supernaturally so, being able to sidestep projectiles and falling masonry with ease. But he noticed that his eyes kept returning to one thing: the black spire.

His own mind was full of dreams of freedom, a strong feeling of hope, that somehow all his grasping, thrashing struggles had led to *this* moment, right now, and he just had to *get there, come on, keep pushing, we've come too far to give up now...*

But for what? Why? He didn't know. Something was eluding him. It was maddening, like he was burrowing blindly through the earth, digging for that shiny mineral vein of *knowledge,* not knowing where he went or why, only that he must get there, he must do whatever needed to be done, he must escape.

Did he plan on hijacking a spacecraft and escaping IV? He didn't even know how feasible that was - he'd never seen one taking off from here. He certainly didn't know how to pilot one, but he'd give it a try. Whatever happened at the end of this journey, he was absolutely certain that the answers lay at the centre of that awful spire; it was a magnet drawing him in, bringing him home.

He passed through the final Rimwall before the Central Wall. There were large crowds pressing all around him; here, it seemed that everybody was trying to get *towards* Central rather than away from it. Many of them held a dangerous urgency in their eyes and held murder in their hearts.

Many, Thaig noticed, were Antennites, wearing their badges with pride - gone was their usual dreamy, hazy demeanour. Whatever was in the air had animated them, too. Some of them were even in full ceremonial garb: those white robes with a single black bar emblazoned on the back of each one. These were usually unseen outside of their gatherings and group meditations.

Everyone, regardless of affiliation, was transfixed by the black spire.

The air positively hummed, vibrated; the air danced; undetectable signals shot through the tight spaces between people. The atmosphere was electric. This couldn't just be the drugs, Thaig told himself, he knew that he'd overdone them but this was *real*; he felt part of the crowd, the swelling, surging mob that sought *something*, none of them were sure what, but *something* was going to happen today to change their lives forever and they were all part of it, all together.

The Central Wall was higher than the others, and the surrounding area was usually crawling with Central security staff. Today it was crawling with Antennites. Thaig had the odd thought that even those who weren't badge-wearing members of the organisation were now walking among them, slavishly marching towards the black pillar, eyes fixed upon it... they were all Antennites now. Had he become one too?

He pulled his hat down further over his eyes, conscious that despite this upheaval, he was a wanted man: more wanted than the average rioter. He could easily be picked out in the crowd.

He looked up at the Central complex, or what he could see of it over the Central Wall. Towering buildings clustered around the base of the black rock spire at their centre. They were pale grey, much like the rest of the architecture of the drab city of Spire, the last grey gypsy-camp of humans huddled at the end of the world.

The tallest buildings were closest to the black pillar, and were built right up against it, possibly chiselled into it. Thinking about this made Thaig's skin crawl, like they'd been hammered into his body; *parasites,* came a thought almost invasively into Thaig's mind, like his flesh had been violated and punctured against his will...

He rubbed his arm reflexively, where he'd torn out the implant. He had changed the bandage when he changed his clothes. The wound was ugly and angry, just like Thaig. He'd tried his best to clean it with a bottle of alcohol that he'd procured from a looted shop. He knew that he needed medical help but he could barely feel the pain. His adrenaline reigned supreme.

That was determined to see this through to the end, regardless of whether his arm withered and fell off or not. He was glad he had a gun now, because he knew his ability to fight would be hampered by his injury. He realised that he didn't even know how to check how much ammunition it had left. He didn't care. Even if it only had one bullet left in the chamber, he would be glad of the opportunity to shoot it at the grey men who hid behind this wall.

He found it hard to stand still, now that the crowd had come to a halt up against the Central Wall; probably a combination of the atmosphere and the extreme amount of drugs he had taken, he thought. His mind raced, his eyes darted back and forth, his jaw wobbled left-to-right.

The crowd became eerily silent. This was the calm before the storm, he thought; that quiet anticipation of chaos. The only sound was the rain and the distant sirens. Thaig pushed and elbowed his way to the front; this was a crowd that could turn ugly at any moment but his sheer size discouraged anybody from trying anything with him. Thaig found that this was often the case - in crowds, in bars, at work... anywhere really.

He tried to get a good view of what was happening at the gate. There was one gate into the Central district, which was always strictly locked down. There were no security staff to be seen, but the gates were tightly shut, with no hope of opening them by any normal means.

Thaig saw that a kind of supply-line was being made by the robe-wearing Antennites, and they were passing things up toward the gate.

Thaig strained to get a closer look. He saw - with alarm - that they were homemade explosives, using materials salvaged from various pieces of equipment, medical supplies, cleaning products and the like... Thaig knew it could be done, from offhand chats with Hubert, but their chats were purely anecdotal. They never actually planned to build bombs for any reason, but here, the Antennites had obviously been doing this for a while. They had built up a veritable arsenal.

There was a sizeable amount of their explosives piling up against the gate. Thaig was less keen to get to the very front of the crowd now; he was very conscious of bomb safety from his time in the mines. This little pile would have a blast radius that would only be able to be described in the subsequent incident report as "irresponsible", and he wasn't as fanatic or brain-dead as the rest of these cultists who were standing around it like sitting ducks.

He saw some stolen mining explosives being passed down too; they wouldn't be able to be detonated so far away from their consoles, but if they were caught in the explosions from the home-made bombs, they would certainly go up with the rest. And then there'd *really* be some fireworks. He fought his way backwards with more gusto.

Funny, he thought, the Antennites must have had sleeper agents within some of the other mining communities, squirrelling away those high-impact mining explosives. None of his lot were Antennites, he was sure of that, but he couldn't speak for the men in the other mines. The Antennites had impressed him; he'd changed his mind about them after seeing what they had achieved. They were still lunatics, obviously, but a different *kind* of lunatic. The violent, revolutionary kind. Not the soft, stupid kind that he had written them off as.

How long had they been planning this?

Had they always been planning this or had the recent strange activity from the spire amped them up?

Was their dreamy demeanour all just a front, so that they could operate their terrorist-cells in secret, or were they genuinely a bunch of hippies that had only recently been radicalised?

Thaig didn't know, and if he didn't get further back into the crowd, he wouldn't be around to find out. He pushed and shoved, causing some aggressive responses from the crowd, but everyone was either focused on the black tower above or on the growing pile of bombs.

Thaig noted that they were trying to set fire to thick rope fuses. A very primitive method, Thaig thought, but he supposed that they were using primitive bombs too. No fancy wireless detonators here. They weren't having much luck setting fire to anything, given the ceaseless rain from above. They obviously hadn't planned on such bad weather. They didn't have long; as soon as enough people in Central realised what was happening outside of their gates, they would co-ordinate a strict response.

This was a violent act of revolution, an act of civil war, and they would come out with whatever tools they had at their disposal. They would all be killed. They had to get this done *now,* he thought, or their chances of getting inside were nil...

Thaig was agitated, he hopped from foot to foot, not knowing what to do. This would all be going smoothly if it would just stop raining and they could light those fuses, he thought... he reached into his pocket and found the pearlescent fragment from the mine, the thing that had started off this incredible chain of events. It had become a sort of talisman to him, a good-luck (or bad-luck) charm. He gripped it hard, and cursed aloud, fixing a furious glance at that horrible black spire in the centre of everything.

If only it would... *stop raining...!*

At this passionate thought, the rain instantly stopped. Incredibly, the clouds above dispersed; a scarcely-believable wind picked up momentarily and then was gone. Thaig was stunned. Did I do that, he asked himself, was that me? Was that the spire? What the hell's going on?

He didn't have much time to think about it, because he saw that the Antennites were running away from the gate, with the fuse on fire and rapidly shortening.

Thaig got as far back as he could and crouched down, hoping that the Antennites in front of him would shield him from the debris.

With a deafening explosion, the gates were punched through. There was a rousing roar from the crowd around him, and they all surged forward, trampling underfoot the piles of sloshing gore and tattered robes which used to be their comrades.

———

Beyond the carnage wrought by the explosion and the shattered gate, Thaig was stunned to see how pleasant everything was behind the Central Wall.

He walked through beautiful leafy gardens, pacified, smelling the sweet nectars and airy floral aromas, so profuse that they managed to overwhelm the stench of burning flesh that lingered in the air behind him. Everything was fresh after the rain. Everything was green, bright, and fragrant. Were it not for the surging crowds of Antennites around him, he would have described it all as peaceful. This place was a haven of life and tranquillity, away from the drab industrial bleakness that made up the rest of the city.

It made him wonder - why? Why had the elites hoarded all of this for themselves, why had there been no effort to brighten up the rest of the city like this? He was shocked at the inequality; he knew that they ate better food in here, drank better booze, had nicer women, but something about these gardens had really irritated Thaig.

As did the lack of Central goons - where *were* they all? Antennites streamed around the gardens, baying for blood, surging towards the tower, kicking down doors and finding... nothing. Nobody.

Either they had all retreated somewhere further within the complex, perhaps a fortress, or a last hold-out... or the entirety of the security forces were out in the wider city, attempting to quell the riots. Thaig found this latter premise hard to believe; surely they would have kept the bulk of the forces here, around the leadership. The leadership, however, were proving hard to find.

Antennites went from building to building, coming out empty-handed, their makeshift weapons bloodless. Eventually they started to pour towards the tallest buildings, the ones around the spire itself. Thaig couldn't actually see the base of it from ground level, it was all fenced off, or had been built directly over. He stared up towards the tower and his mind swam. Something felt off. Were they about to be ambushed?

But by whom? From where would they come?

Was this whole place fake, Thaig wondered, a kind of potemkin village designed to pacify the folk outside? The gardens were nice, but the buildings... empty, pointless? What went on here, behind the highest wall? Where were the government? Where were their cronies?

He heard footsteps behind him; his right arm went to the gun in his breast-pocket. He turned around slowly, nonchalantly, expecting danger but not wanting to give the game away before he had eyes on his opponent.

He saw - to his surprise - Hubert the dodgy doctor. The thin man looked even thinner, and he had a black eye. His face was covered with bruises and cuts. Hubert was not a fighting man, so Thaig knew something was wrong. He had no idea what the doctor could be doing here, but he sensed no threat from him, so his hand left the gun alone.

Hubert said, with a wry smile, "I'd have known you anywhere, Thaig. There's only one freakishly gigantic man I know that moves around so... *shiftily*. The hat's doing nothing to disguise you. You'd need a shrink-ray."

Thaig removed the hat. It was annoying him anyway.

"Don't suppose you've got any cigarettes?" Hubert asked, "return the favour?"

Thaig shook his head.

Hubert looked at the top of Thaig's head and frowned. He said, "Do you dye that mop of yours bright ginger? Didn't know you were going grey."

"What?" Thaig said, taken aback. He'd never touched a bottle of hair dye in his life.

"You're going grey, man, you've got whitish-grey hair in the centre of your head. You know, the roots. You've got grey roots."

Thaig pondered, wide-eyed, playing with the fragment in his pocket. Roots, he thought to himself, *root*, where had he heard that recently...

"Silent treatment again, is it?" Hubert looked around. "Could have told me you were a wanted man, Thaig. That's just common courtesy. Central goons dragged me out of bed and brought me here a few hours ago, started roughing me up until I told them everything about you. Not that I had much to tell 'em. I had to tell them about the stims, though... I'll never work again.

"Although, with what your friends here are up to, looks like none of us ever will. There'll be no jobs left after Spire goes up in flames. What's going on here, big man? Sounds like the whole city's gone mad. Just what have you got yourself wrapped up in?"

Thaig looked him straight in the eyes and said, absolutely sincerely, "I have no idea, Hubert. I have absolutely no idea. They've tried to kill me - twice - since we last met. I'm here to find out exactly what's going on, and... and..." He trailed off.

"And?"

"And... I don't know. I just feel like I have to be here. I have to dig and find out what's hidden beneath all this, Hubert, I don't know, I guess its the stims, or the stress, or both, but I've been losing my grip, man, I don't know what's real or not, did you see how it stopped raining there? I did that, Hubert, I swear-"

"The spire, eh? Got to you too?" Hubert interrupted him. "Everyone's gone completely mad, and I think it's the activity from the tower."

"No, listen to me," Thaig said, exasperated, "it's something more. I found this- this- *thing,* and next thing I know I'm setting off bombs and shouting at the rain-"

Hubert cut in again. "Yep, sounds like the kind of nonsense I've been hearing all day. I can't even look at the bloody thing without getting a headache either, Thaig, I can't even think straight... it's like my thoughts aren't my own. That might be the head injuries, too, mind you."

Thaig gave up. Obviously Hubert wasn't going to help him. He looked at the purple bruises and red, angry cuts which covered his face. "I'm sorry, Hubert, but at least you're alive. They killed my whole team, you know. Killed them, all dead."

"I'm sorry to hear that, Thaig. Looks like they're going to get their comeuppance today though, eh?"

Thaig grunted. "Say, Hubert? Where the hell are they all, anyway? The Central lot?"

Hubert shrugged and said, "I don't know. There were only two with me. I had a bag over my head until I was inside one of these buildings. Next thing I know, your friends in the robes were untying me. I've treated Antennites before, mostly chemical burns and minor blast injuries. I think some of them play with explosives. One of them recognised me, anyway - just as well he did, because those lot are out for blood, I can tell. Didn't know you were with 'em, Thaig."

"I was just tagging along, I suppose," Thaig said. "They were going where I was going. I still think they're a bunch of freaks."

Hubert laughed. "Have you had a look in the mirror lately, Thaig?"

"Leave it out. I've had a hell of a night."

"You going easy on the stims?"

"Eh..." Thaig trailed off again, chewing his lip.

"So you just wandered towards the spire when everything kicked off, huh? And you don't know why? You sure you ain't an Antennite? What happened while I was in there, anyway?"

Thaig thought better of telling him about the bombs he'd set off, the mine collapse he'd caused, the people he'd killed... "Long story," he said.

There were noises from their left. They watched a gang of disappointed Antennites come pouring from out of one of the tallest cone-shaped buildings that had been built right against the Spire. They made their way eagerly to the next one, and started to break down its doors. More Antennites ran around aimlessly, looking for things to smash and people to maim.

"Well," said Hubert, "Nothing good's going to happen here. And you're as talkative as ever. I'm off - going underground."

"To the mines?" asked Thaig.

"No, you big lummox. I'm going into hiding. I'll never work as a legitimate doctor again, will I? I'll have to reach out to some of my less... salubrious associates. Thanks for that, Thaig. You're a bad man to know."

Thaig looked at him and shrugged. "Sorry."

"Ah, don't worry about it, the whole place is going to hell anyway. None of this was your fault, as far as I know. I'll have to get this implant out, too, I suppose. Just as well I have a stash of anaesthetics."

Thaig rolled up his sleeve to show his bandaged left arm and grinned maniacally. "Lucky for some," he said.

Hubert just laughed again and shook his head. He started to walk away, back towards the gate that led to the rest of the city. He shouted over his shoulder, "You owe me a cigarette, you big mad bastard," before he picked up his pace into a jog.

Thaig turned around and looked at the spire, lost in thought. His head was still buzzing. Sometimes he could see a milky, pearlescent swirl around the edges of his vision, but he wasn't convinced that it was really there. He hadn't slept for a long time, and he was completely strung out on Hubert's pills.

He watched the Antennites stream into the next

building and begin surging up toward the top of the tall conical tower-building.

Thaig wasn't convinced that the answer lay *upward* at all... the Antennites seemed to want to get as close to the tip of that black spire as possible, but something was pulling him in quite the opposite direction. He remembered Hubert's comment about going underground. He had to go down... to get at the *root* of the issue.

He could see, tucked away against one of the buildings next to the spire, a much smaller version of the mining elevators used in places like Mine 9. He walked onto it and pushed the button. The door-panels emerged from the floor and closed around him immediately - all security checks had been disabled here. They obviously weren't expecting anybody without authorisation to get this far.

He had no idea where the elevator led. He rested his hand on the gun in his jacket, and the platform began to descend. His other hand gripped the shiny fragment tightly, which he realised he'd been doing unconsciously for a long time. He ground his jaw and tried to ignore the invasive thoughts that plagued his mind and the shifting white hues that bordered his vision.

Thaig emerged into a gigantic cavern, at least half a mile across and hollow in the middle. It was lit by the same mining lights they used in Mine 9. He stood on a ring-shaped balcony walkway, which was carved into the outer wall. He recognised that this had been done by advanced mining equipment. In the centre was the black spire, which disappeared into the ceiling. Thaig had never considered that the long black part of the rock might stretch so far below ground, but there it was; even longer and more horrible than Thaig had ever imagined. It seemed to be wider down here, and its mass was studded with what looked like probes, each adorned with little blinking lights.

Thaig peered over the edge of the balcony to see how long the spire was, but he couldn't see where it ended. He gasped. The cavern was incredibly deep. The spire went all the way down. It disappeared beneath a ring-shaped metallic platform, suspended from the walls by hooked wires on its outer edge with the black spire going through its centre. He could see that the cavern continued downward past the platform, but he couldn't see past that ring.

On the platform, he could see men in grey uniforms running back and forth. So *this* was where they were hiding, he thought. It was oddly silent in the cavern - they clearly moved with some urgency, but there was no shouting, no beeping alarms or sirens like those on the surface. There were flashing lights, red and orange, bathing the cavern in a warm glow, but no accompanying noises.

The balcony he stood on tapered off at one end, into a walkway which spiralled downwards, carved out from the edges of the cavern. Thaig made his way down it, and the air became noticeably warmer. Thaig could see cameras everywhere - he didn't care. Nobody seemed to be coming for him. He kept his eyes peeled for hidden ledges where he might be sniped from, and blind corners cut into the rock beside the walkway. There were plenty, but they were all empty. Thaig was almost disappointed. He had itchy fists, he wanted to pound skulls, tear limbs, rip out throats - he sucked in air through his grinding teeth and tried to calm down.

If he shot first, there would be no asking questions later, and these Central scum had some answering to do.

He reached the bottom, and paused behind a corner before walking over the ring-platform. He could see an elevator at the far end, which led further downward into the deep cavern, as well as a great number of screens and consoles. Down here, the black spire was a much paler shade of grey, and it was much wider. It looked somehow softer, less rocky than the black protrusion above the ground. The warning-lights bathed the scene in flashes of orange and red. There was a flurry of activity, with heavy boots clanking over the metal surface, and people talking in low murmurs.

Thaig stained to hear them; they talked of the situation up on the surface, they talked of the situation "below", they reported statistics and read out numbers from screens, but Thaig couldn't hear the details. He could hear them repeating a singular mantra: "Don't panic. Keep cool, keep calm." He peeked out and squinted, trying to identify who was stood at the largest console giving out orders to the rest.

"Bastard," he swore, under his breath.

Mulberry.

Somehow, he'd survived the collapse of Mine 9 and

beaten him here. Thaig supposed that there could be entrances to this facility from anywhere; Central guard stations, Rimwalls, sewer-gratings... he could have gotten here by a multitude of methods. He looked bad; his face was swollen and patched, and one of his arms was in a sling. Thaig was happy that he hadn't escaped unscathed, at least, but he'd much rather Mulberry was dead.

Thaig drew the gun. There was still time for that.

There was a hundred feet of bare platform between him and the large console that his nemesis stood beside. There was no sneaking the rest of the way. Thaig was too big for hiding anyway, and it wasn't his style. He was sick of sneaking. So he did what he did best: he stood up straight, stretched out his back and shoulders, and marched right up the middle of the platform, bold as brass.

There were frowns from those around him, but he simply kept his eyes focused on Mulberry, gun in hand. Nobody seemed to want to stop him. His presence was causing confusion, but nobody seemed to be able to tear themselves away from the screens they were monitoring. Thaig reached the console which Mulberry stood at completely un-apprehended.

"BASTARD!" Thaig shouted, and held up the gun.

Every face on the platform turned toward him, including Mulberry's.

"Thaig," said Mulberry in a low voice, "it's *very* important that you remain calm. Violence now will cause... it will kill us all, Thaig. It'll kill everybody in Spire."

"I'm real tired of the riddles," Thaig growled. "Somebody better tell me *everything* or I'll happily do whatever I have to do to bring this cavern down on our heads."

"Don't panic. Keep cool, keep calm," said Mulberry.

Thaig punched him in the face.

He'd heard enough of that nonsense already. He found that there was rarely a better way to emphasise his desire for a quick resolution than to simply punch somebody in the face.

Mulberry fell back on the console. From below, there came an abyssal groaning, so deep that it hurt Thaig's eardrums and made his whole body vibrate, and the platform swung from left to right. Rather than try to hold Thaig back or jump on him, Mulberry's subordinates held their arms out and shook their heads, as though trying to defuse the situation. They murmured words of placation and cessation.

"Tell me what's going on or I'll shoot you," Thaig said matter-of-factly.

Mulberry stood up and wiped his bloody nose on his sling.

"Thaig," Mulberry said, "I will explain everything. You've done very well to get down here, and without your slobbering Antennite associates too. But you *must* remain calm, or the whole city's done. Before I explain, though," Mulberry sniffed and then spat out bloody phlegm, "I want you to know that I never liked you, and if the situation was any different, I would have you killed in an instant."

Thaig laughed. "Feeling's mutual, Mulberry. I've

been telling everybody who'll listen that you're a hard-faced, snooty, stuck-up bastard for years."

"I know," Mulberry said. "We monitor everything, remember?"

"You enjoy snooping on people's private moments, do ya, Mulberry?"

"Not overly. Most people's lives are *shockingly* dull."

"You're right there," Thaig conceded. "Enough pleasantries, anyway. Tell me what this is, tell me what it's doing." He gestured towards the large console and towards the wide spire structure at the centre of the cavern.

"Would you kindly get that gun out of my face before I do so? It is having more than a small effect on my ability to keep calm."

Thaig grinned his trademark maniacal grin and said, "No."

Mulberry took a breath before he began. He pointed at the console before him. "You see this?"

Thaig looked. In his pocket, he gripped his lucky charm, his lodestone of trouble, his bright white fragment from the mine. It was hot, and it was softer now. Holding it felt good. Like scratching an itch underneath the skin of his palm. He gripped it tightly, until his knuckles hurt; he felt like he'd need all the good-luck charms in the world to avoid losing his cool while this vast network of lies and oppression was unwound before him.

On the screen, there was the image of a vertical tube; a long, thin shape, outlined in white, coiled up at the bottom and tapering off to a point at the top. There were numerous dots all the way down it, with numbers and percentages constantly flickering and changing, and various annotations with lines pointing to different parts of the structure. There were rings around it, five of them, at various points, and one flat horizontal line near the top of it, intersecting it nearly at its tip.

There was a flicker of recognition, but Mulberry interrupted Thaig's natural cognitive process to point out the obvious solution that he would have arrived at himself only moments later, as was Mulberry's habit. Thaig hated him.

"You're looking at the spire, Thaig, the black tower in the centre of our city, Spire... the last city on this accursed planet."

Thaig nodded. He had many questions but that had answered none of them.

"W-"

"You will have many questions," Mulberry interrupted.

"W- yes," Thaig started - he *hated* this annoying man, he really did. "Don't interrupt me again, Mulberry, as long as we both live. That is *crucial* if you wish for me to keep calm, and if you wish for your face to remain unmolested by bullets."

Mulberry raised an eyebrow sarcastically.

"That horizontal line near the top of the spire, that's the surface, isn't it? This thing goes *that* far down?"

"Indeed," said Mulberry.

"And that coil at the bottom?"

"We've excavated that far down and that's what we

found. It was the first thing our grandparents did when they got here, which shouldn't surprise you given the mysterious nature of this thing. The structure ends in a kind of coil."

"What is it?"

Mulberry took a deep breath. "It's... alive, Thaig. It's alive. You're looking at the shape of its *body*."

Thaig nodded. He was shocked, but several signs had been pointing toward this; it felt "right" to him, like everything was clicking into place in a satisfying manner, like the pieces of a jigsaw puzzle. There were still several gaps in the overall picture, though.

"And the spire above the surface? That's just a protrusion?"

"Indeed. There are no known examples of this species anywhere else in the universe, but there must be more. 'Chicken or the egg' and all that. We assume that it burrows down when young, or is born here, or hatches here, you understand, and sends out a kind of... antenna."

Thaig snorted. "Those kook Antennites had it right all along, then? It's alive, and what we can see from the surface is an antenna!"

"No, not exactly. They see it as their deity, as their saviour... apparently with no knowledge that it even extends underground, actually. In some ways, it could be our saviour, but it could just as easily be our doom. That's what all this is about, Thaig; ensuring the former rather than the latter."

"So it's just some dumb alien? Why all of the secrecy, the lies, the murder, then? What aren't you telling me?"

Mulberry sighed. "You have noticed the strange psychic effects it has on people, yes? Surely you must have noticed it yourself?"

"A little. Nothing too extreme," Thaig lied.

Mulberry raised his eyebrow again doubtfully. "I'm sure. Well, Thaig, we surmise that it's this creature's primary survival mechanism... its defence mechanism. We cannot know how creatures such as this would 'normally' behave, as it's the only one we know of, but it *does* seem capable of manipulating both psychical and physical phenomena."

Thaig nodded along. "A defence mechanism, you say... against what? The extremes of this horrible little planet?"

"In the case of the physical manipulation, yes. We suspect that it calms the land around it while it gestates, to keep itself safe. There have been no earthquakes here - *despite* your best efforts - and the storms which wrack the rest of the planet are suspiciously absent around Spire. And it's cool and wet and fertile - you might have noticed the rain?"

Thaig thought better of telling Mulberry about him stopping the rain on the surface... it still could have been a coincidence, Thaig convinced himself uneasily. He let Mulberry continue.

"The rain stopped just there, uncharacteristically suddenly. It was accompanied by a large, anomalous psychic signal, the likes of which we have never seen. We are unsure of the link between them. Surely, the manipulation of the weather - of the physical - is its defence mechanism against this strange little planet. The psychic phenomena, on the other hand, we can only assume is its defence mechanism against... us."

"Makes sense. We've got it trapped in a cave after all."

"Indeed."

"Why... why do we have it trapped in a cave, exactly?"

"Another defence mechanism, Thaig, of course. Ours. Our survival mechanism. If it leaves, the resulting upheaval of earth will kill most of the residents of Spire. The remaining miserable survivors will be swept away by whatever arrives next. Lightning storms? Dust storms? Boiling hot tornadoes? Lava cascades? You name it. It keeps them all away while it gestates, as I said. It calms the physical atmosphere around it."

Thaig was silent, comprehending everything. He supposed, begrudgingly, that what Mulberry was saying made sense. They were all kept alive by the creature down here.

"But why the oppression?" Thaig asked, exasperated, "why not just tell everybody the truth? What is it that *you lot* are actually doing down here? Keeping it alive?"

"What we do here is a massive psychical manipulation experiment, Thaig. What we have found is that the psychic phenomena can be reversed, to go in the *opposite direction...* in other words, human thought, human emotion, human states of mind can influence the creature."

Thaig frowned. "Explains you wanting me to keep calm," he said, "and those tranquil gardens you have grown in the innermost part of the city?"

"Very astute, yes. This is partly the reason for separating the majority of the population away from the centre - proximity has a large effect. This close to the creature, if we are angry, if we do harm, if we are violent, it could thrash and lash out. We would be dead in an instant."

"And it would potentially escape, you think?"

"Almost certainly. It remains in a kind of dazed stupor. We have been tracking its growth - by which I mean *us*, the human population, the whole time we have been settled here. It stopped growing decades ago. It's done - it's ready to pop. We're keeping it repressed, through a kind of psychic oppression, until we can make it off this rock."

"What do you mean, 'make it off this rock'? Can't we all just get in a ship and go? Why can't we just get a message out to the offworlders to come and rescue us, and stop this horrible charade?"

"It's not that easy, Thaig... we haven't the materials or know-how to build new ships. All our old stock was lost in the calamities which destroyed the rest of the colonies on IV. We are - and stay calm when I tell you this - stranded, for the time being."

Thaig's stomach sank. He felt the creature beneath him growl and roar, and the platform swung violently. A few of Mulberry's silent subordinates fell to one knee or leaned on the console to steady themselves. A part of the screen which showed the full length of the creature flashed and several exclamation marks were displayed.

"I said stay calm, Thaig, please - take a deep breath. You're a big boy, you can handle it. You do everything alone, right? You're an island already, Thaig. You never needed anybody to come and rescue you. Nothing's changed. Keep calm."

Thaig smiled and nodded. Sadly, Mulberry was correct, despite his obvious attempt at flattery and placation. The platform steadied.

"That's it... good," said Mulberry in soothing tones. "You think *you're* oppressed? We live in a constant state of psycho-terrorism down here... it's all smiles, all day!"

His flippancy angered Thaig but he kept a handle on it for his own safety. "We *are* oppressed, yes," he said, "and some of you take a bit too much pleasure in that, Mulberry."

"Those who take pleasure in their job are often the best candidates, Thaig. The cream - or as I'm sure you'd put it, the scum - rises to the top."

Thaig snorted. "I'll give you that one."

"An oppressed population, one that knows it isn't going anywhere until some sort of vague goal is reached... wandering around, dreamily, doing repetitive tasks, never rocking the boat...this was all carefully crafted, Thaig. By our great-grandparents and all those who came after. Remember that the psychic link to the creature goes both ways."

"The *creature* feels oppressed, then," Thaig realised aloud, "the creature feels like it's not going anywhere, until we reach our goal... which is what, exactly? Mining quotas?"

"I cannot trust you with that information."

"I have a gun pointed at your face, Mulberry. You can trust me with *anything*."

"You are mentally unstable, Thaig. Given time, we will tell you the rest, but you can't handle it right now, do you understand? And your inability to handle it will kill us all."

Thaig sighed. He really didn't want to have to kill Mulberry until he knew everything, and he still had so much more to learn.

"So, we keep it trapped in a kind of nightmare, then? Struggling to wake up and break free?" Thaig realised that the desire for freedom, the writhing, the wriggling, that frustrating feeling of trying to break free but never knowing *why* or *from what*... that was the creature's feelings being beamed back at him from its black antenna. He ruminated. What a horrible thought-loop they were all stuck in; the human population of Spire and this incomprehensible alien creature, all trapped in a coma-dream of cosmic proportions.

He felt an overwhelming wave of sympathy for the poor thing.

"We're just here to study this thing, right?" Thaig said. "The mining, the colonisation, all of that was just a facade to come and study this thing that the offworlders found on this deathtrap of a planet. Right? They wanted the mines just to search for more of them, or search for eggs, or something?"

Mulberry sighed. "If only that were the case, Thaig. If only."

Thaig lowered the gun. He was quite confident that

they wouldn't bother killing him after he'd made it this far and knew this much. Also, he thought, the violence of his murder might wake the creature and get them all killed anyway.

"I can handle it, Mulberry," he said, "just tell me."

"You can't right now, Thaig, I promise. You need a long sleep, and by the looks of it, a long and thorough detox beforehand."

"I'll find out, I promise you that. I don't care if I have to kill you first, I'll find it out from one of your stooges here. Tell me something else, then."

"Yes?"

"The vein - the thing you call a root - the thing my men found in Mine 9. Why did you kill them after finding it? Why did I need to die, why did you have men waiting for me when I got home?"

"Can you keep a cool head? I sympathise, Thaig, I really do. I would be furious in your place. I'm worried that *you* will be furious when discussing the deaths of your men. Remember, also, that you killed plenty of mine in Mine 9. I'm being sensible enough to keep calm about that."

Thaig took a deep breath and tried to adopt an attitude of mental numbness; the detachment common to soldiers, doctors, and murderers everywhere. "I'm not the delicate flower I may seem to be on the surface, Mulberry."

"I hope not. The roots - those pearly 'veins' that may be found underground in the mines... this alien specimen puts them out. We hadn't seen one for years, but we think that the creature must have worked on this one for a long time, sending out a long, thin, snaking tentacle out through the earth and all the way to Mine 9."

"How didn't you detect it before?"

"We haven't mined out the area underneath it, exactly; it's unsafe to dig so deep. And there'd be no way to suspend it otherwise, without it resting on the floor of the cavern."

"Ah - a potentially rude awakening if it dropped down?"

"Indeed. It sends out a root from *underneath* itself; in this case it went all the way out there to Mine 9. These roots contain an intense concentration of the creature's vitality. You can think of it as its lifeblood - our eyes detect it in the visual spectrum as a sort of shifting pearlescence. The black spire above ground can be thought of as dead tissue - it's still attached to the creature, but it's more like a horn, more like dead bone. Dead tissue, and yet still highly conductive of its bioelectrical signals."

"That's why it gets less black on the way down?"

"Yes. Further down, the colouring approaches the pearlescent shifting shades of the root that you found."

"Why the murder, though? You're avoiding that question, Mulberry. Don't make me get angry - tell me."

"Thaig, you don't know what happens to people who come into contact with those roots. They appear to be the creature's desperate attempts at freeing itself from its 'coma dream'. An intense psychic influence is placed over anybody that touches the root substance, or takes a piece of it for themselves, or consumes it, or whatever. You should be aware that this is some of the most heavily suppressed information of all, Thaig.

"In the past, this influence has manifested in extremely erratic behaviour. Up to and including the intentional sabotage of the city of Spire, which we can only guess is the creature's heavy-handed attempt to stop our operation and free itself. Such highly concentrated 'lifeblood' can utterly dominate the psyche of the average human."

"Everyone I've ever known, everyone I've heard of, that's gone 'off-world'…"

"Yes. Gone mad and neutralised by Central, most likely. Or brought into the fold - occasionally somebody finds out too much without coming under its influence, at which point they're more useful working down here than reclining up in the graveyards."

"What about me? Couldn't I have been useful?"

"You… could have, yes…" Mulberry shifted uneasily.

Thaig laughed, delighted with the simplicity of his realisation: "But you just don't like me, do you?"

Mulberry froze, wide-eyed.

"Don't worry, Mulberry, I'm not angry. The feeling's mutual, remember? If I could have ordered your assassination to avoid working with you, I'd have done it in a heartbeat."

"Well," said Mulberry, relaxing, "it certainly is refreshing to have it out like this. Maybe we could have been friends after all."

There came a shout from above. The cavern rumbled and dust and stones shook from the ceiling.

The Antennites had found the elevator.

———

The cavern shook and the spire before them shuddered left to right, wriggling almost imperceptibly, but it moved a *lot* more than the operatives who kept it under their psychic thrall wanted it to. The men in grey ran to and fro, not knowing what to do. They could surrender and be murdered by a mob of crazed cultists, all under the influence of the very thing they tried to suppress. If they took up arms and fought back, well... the creature could wake up, and then *everyone* died.

"Retreat to the next ring!" Mulberry shouted.

Thaig looked at the screen again and saw the five ring-shaped platforms. He looked further down, towards the coil. He could see a circular shape, set aside, below the fifth ring, just slightly above the coiled lengths of the strange creature that lay at the bottom of the cavern. Looking at the relative size of the spire protruding from the surface - *tiny* - this cavern must descend for tens of miles.

Mulberry hobbled towards the elevator at the other end of the ring platform. Thaig easily kept pace beside him.

"Sorry about the leg, Mulberry."

"This wasn't you, believe it or not," Mulberry said. "*Your* injuries are mostly limited to my upper body. Some rioter hit me in the knee with a length of pipe after I crawled out of your office."

"How'd you get away from him?"

"I stabbed him."

Thaig grunted. Fair enough, he thought.

He looked up at the spiral ramp that led up to the surface elevator. It was, as he expected, absolutely teeming with Antennites, most of them in white robes. The air was thicker than ever with that electric feeling, that essence of *potential,* which felt like it could all erupt into flames and bright lightning at a moment's notice.

Thaig's vision swam. He'd been gripping his little fragment the whole time, hidden in his pocket, and he could fully see little white pearly lines swimming into his field of vision now. He thought better of revealing this to Mulberry after his revelation - was he really under the influence of the creature?

Of course he was; weren't they all, to some extent?

He wanted the creature to be free. If he could work out a way to do that without killing everybody in Spire, then he would take that path. But he couldn't do anything without knowing all of the facts, so he decided to ride along with Mulberry until he found out the rest. He was still in charge though, he reminded himself: he still had the gun in his hand.

His sympathy towards the creature was *almost* beginning to eclipse his sympathy for his own kind; they were half-dead here anyway. Zombies, shambling around, digging at the ground. Spire was this planet's little mushroom-farm: the people were kept in the dark and fed bullshit. The creature, on the other hand, was a glorious, multifaceted, infinitely complex alien being, capable of influencing the world around it - and even the psychic plane - by mysterious means.

And it was kept trapped in the ground, in an infinite, horrible, black nightmare, constantly struggling for freedom. By *them*. The pointless parasites on the surface: the *humans*.

The floor shook beneath him as the creature stirred.

He needed to get to the root of this. There was something he still hadn't found out from Mulberry: why couldn't they just leave? If the offworlders didn't even care about the creature, why couldn't they come and collect their colonists? A lot had gone very wrong here; the IV mining colony project was an absolute disaster; the planet was completely inhospitable to human life despite its water and occasional temperate climate; and yet they'd found something *very* interesting. An alien. A bright, brilliant alien species capable of so much...

They reached the elevator.

"There aren't many of you left, are there?" Thaig asked. "You Central lot? The inner district was deserted."

"No. We're very short-staffed. The men we do have are mostly down here, on these five ring-platforms. We've been keen to keep that a secret, and until your recent escapades, we were doing a good job."

"You certainly had me fooled. You in charge here then, Mulberry? I haven't seen anybody giving you orders. You lot always did keep the leadership pretty well hidden."

Mulberry limped onto the platform, grunting with

pain. "I might be, actually," he said, as though the thought had just occurred to him.

"What do you mean?"

"The creature has been making our leaders kill themselves."

"Ah. Figures." Thaig didn't need much more explanation than that... of course it had been. It made perfect sense that it would go for the leadership first, and try to corrupt their thoughts and feelings.

"Yes. It's grim work down here. I may very well be next in the leadership hierarchy, in which case yes, I'm in charge."

"Sounds like the job nobody wants, eh?"

"Indeed. Leadership usually comes with some perks, doesn't it, but here..."

"Here, a gigantic alien creature is more likely to invade your thoughts and drive you to suicide?"

"Precisely. I don't feel like killing myself just yet, Thaig, so I've got one up on the damned thing for now."

"Well, congratulations on the promotion."

"Very funny. Are you coming aboard the elevator or what?"

Thaig stepped onto the elevator platform. There was space for some of Mulberry's men, and they were making their way over, retreating before the cultist horde which bayed for their blood.

Thaig leaned forward and smashed the emergency override button.

Door-panels appeared from the floor and enclosed the

elevator platform. The panels closed in the dismayed grey faces of the grey-suited men.

"What are you doing, you madman?" said Mulberry, trying not to betray his angry disbelief. "We could have saved them- oh. I see."

Thaig had the gun pointing into Mulberry's ribcage.

"We're not going to the next ring down, Mulberry."

"No?"

"We're going down as far as this thing goes."

"Thaig! I'm warning you!"

"On your console, I saw a small antechamber below the ring platforms. Take me there."

"That is... unwise."

"Take me there."

Mulberry sighed and pressed a button on a small panel, using his implant's security clearance to bypass the various red symbols and signs which the screen spat out.

"You'll kill us all, Thaig."

"Maybe," Thaig said nonchalantly.

"You don't care? And *we're* supposed to be the evil ones?"

"I'm beginning to think we're all bad guys, Mulberry. What we're doing to that creature is... evil. Cruel."

"Remember what I said about those who come into contact with the roots, Thaig? Do you think your brief exposure might be having an effect on the way that you're thinking?"

Slowly, Thaig withdrew his left hand from his pocket and opened it, revealing the small piece of the root that he held.

Mulberry's eyes widened, and so did Thaig's own. The fragment had dug halfway into the palm of his hand, with the skin melding into the pearlescent fragment. Shocked, he tried to shake it loose, but couldn't; it was part of him now. His arm tingled; he ordered Mulberry to remove the bandage from his implant wound. Mulberry did so in numb silence.

Where Thaig expected to see angry redness and the raw meat of his inner forearm exposed to the surface, he instead saw glittering white pearlescence, which filled the wound like resin poured into a hollow sculpture. He moved his hand and arm under the lights in the elevator, marvelling at the hues which shifted back and forth, much like the emotional feedback loops between the humans and the creature, back and forth, back and forth, misery and joy, suppression and desire, oppression and freedom, back and forth.

"Well," murmured Thaig, "even I wasn't expecting this... have you ever seen anything like it?"

"You should have told me about this," Mulberry said.

"Wouldn't you have just had me killed on the spot?"

"I felt like doing that as soon as I saw the roots in your hair. A telltale sign, but I couldn't be sure. You are getting old, after all. We'd best get comfortable, Thaig. It's a long way down."

―――

The elevator came to a halt some minutes later. Mulberry lead the way out, and Thaig followed close behind while the cavern rumbled and shook around them. They could no longer hear the battle above; they were too far down, but Thaig could safely assume that the Antennites had had their way, and were busy murdering and smashing things to their hearts' content.

The creature stirred and moaned. It was indeed a lot more colourful down here. There were pearly whites, pulsing warm oranges, blending into visceral reds and pinks... Looking directly at the central column made his brain fizz; the coloured edges of his vision flashed; electric pulses massaged his brain as though saying *yes, yes, more, keep going, nearly there...*

This part of the cavern was older and less well-maintained. Thaig was shocked at how thick the thing's body was down here; there was no room for a ring platform around it. The width of the cavern was almost all taken up by the creature's tubular body. He looked down to see the beginning of a coiled mass, the top of the pile of the rest of the creature's carapace. It pulsated and flashed with red hot boiling energy. It shifted slightly, but returned to its original position.

Trapped.

He shook his head. This all felt so wrong... They had imprisoned it. He watched its colourful coiled body stir and felt the whole cavern heave; his heavy heart heaved in return. A large, bass-filled noise made his head rattle; whether it was the creature crying out or the very earth around him screaming, he had no way of knowing.

He ordered Mulberry to disable the elevator behind them. He didn't want to be followed. There was an old blast-door leading to a room recessed in the cavern wall, just off to the side of the creature. Thaig gestured towards it, and Mulberry approached the panel.

"Are you sure, Thaig? What you see in here will change you."

"I'm sure, Mulberry. Nothing can shock me any more."

"That's what I said, too... yet I still wasn't prepared for it. Before I do this, let me ask you one thing: are you really prepared to kill us all?" Mulberry genuinely sounded fearful and sad. "Because if so, shoot me now. I won't do it alive. You can unlock the door with my implant, but it'll be with my dead corpse's hand; I won't be the one who wilfully lets you destroy Spire."

"If you had given me answers upstairs, we wouldn't even be down here," Thaig said. "I need to know why we can't just get off this rock. Why we can't *both* live in peace, by which I mean us and this alien. We can leave, go *home*... our real home. Off-world. And the creature can leave and find its own kind... we can take data about this creature back and be heroes. We've found something far better than poxy old *globalt*! Alien life!"

"Thaig..." Mulberry sighed. "It seems that your intentions are pure enough, despite the root being a part of you now. I'll let you in, but there are further explanations required."

"Good! That's all I've been asking you for all damn day!"

Mulberry opened the door and they stepped inside.

"Thaig... welcome to the Chamber of the First Root."

They had emerged into the small antechamber of the cavern, which was lit by the shining white root at its centre. It was thicker than the one that Thaig's men had found and he could see that it stretched all the way back towards the centre of the cavern, where it disappeared through the back wall and presumably led back to the creature at the centre of Spire.

Thaig looked around the room's cavalcade of strange features. Spilling out from the root were more rocky shapes, all shining white like the root; Thaig couldn't make out what they were yet. Was the root expanding into the rest of the chamber? Was it pushing outwards?

He walked toward the room's centre. His eyes became accustomed to the shifting hues and odd lighting and the shapes became more distinct, although he still couldn't make out what they were. He leaned closer and peered into one of the lumpen masses that protruded from the root... and it peered back at him.

He reeled backwards.

"Mulberry! What the hell is this!" he shouted. The cavern rocked from side to side in response to his emotional outburst.

"Shhhh... calm," whispered Mulberry in return. "Remember? Calm."

Thaig looked at the horrific mass in front of him. Stretched out within the white pearly material were the unmistakable features of a man's face, but the proportions were wrong. It was like the man had been boiled down into some hideous stew, and the different parts of his face had bobbed to the surface, and the whole thing had been allowed to cool and congeal into some goopy human mess. One eye was dead and inactive, but the other fixed Thaig with a piercing milky gaze.

Thaig felt sick. He span around and saw that the cavern was full of them; he saw eyes everywhere, staring back at him, and his head whirled. He wanted to scream. He had never even imagined anything so sick and horrific. To have to face it like this was disgusting and disorienting. Everywhere he looked he saw hands, heads, eyes, mouths - all stretched or compressed to oblivion.

He fell to one knee and tried to keep from vomitting.

"Mulberry... is this going to happen to me?" He held up his hand, with the root fragment embedded in it.

"Not necessarily, Thaig. Not if you choose not to."

"I... I rather emphatically choose not to, Mulberry, you mad bastard! What do I have to do? Chop my hand off? Say the word, get a knife, let's do this!" Thaig waved his hand around frantically.

"Let me explain what this cavern is, before we remove any limbs. You are in no *immediate* danger."

"Alright. Did these... things... were they people, once?"

"I'd like to think that they still are," Mulberry said. "When we first realised the nature of this creature, and the psychic link shared between us, some of the first overseers decided to remain down here, in meditation. Silent, forceful projection of feelings of peace, of domination, of pacification... it worked, but their contact with the root has done this to them over time. Some of the least... human... 'shapes' that you see are of the founding generation of Spire. They've been here the longest. We call these people in here the Pacifiers."

Thaig was revolted. Fascinated, but revolted. He felt like he was watching a grisly surgery; his stomach turned, but he was enthralled. He wanted to know what all those gory parts were, he wanted to know what each organ did, he wanted all the pieces of the puzzle. He'd come this far.

"I'd call them freaks," he said.

"Most distasteful. Look at them, Thaig, look into their eyes. They have made the ultimate sacrifice. These Pacifiers have given up their very humanity, doomed themselves to a potentially immortal existence of... *this*. To keep Spire safe until we make it off-world. They've sacrificed themselves for the people of Spire."

Thaig looked around. He could see that many of the shapes in the Cavern of the First Root were half-encrusted; some sat up in asana-meditation positions, some reclined against flat patches of rock as though they lay on hammocks, some simply leaned against the walls. Others were just... shimmering goop.

"Nothing is worth this. Just end it, Mulberry. Look at what we're doing here. This is sick. This whole colony - this planet - is a mistake. Let's just end it now."

"You might have ended it anyway, with your stunt in Mine 9. Your friends upstairs are causing psychic disturbances that the Pacifiers here may not be able to iron out. I may have to sit down and join them... I hoped I never would, but they need all the help they can get."

"That's psychic terrorism..."

"It's *survival*, Thaig. Potentially, the survival of all

humanity. It's absolutely crucial that we get off-world. We can maybe make rudimentary spacecraft with materials from the mines-"

"Wait," Thaig said, "what do you mean, the survival of all humanity? We're just a colony."

"Place your hand upon the root, Thaig."

"Hell no!"

"You won't be enveloped, Thaig. The encrustation process takes years."

"I don't trust you."

"Why would I want you to incorporate into the Cavern in your current confused and adversarial mental state? Place your hand upon it, close your eyes, and you will see."

Mulberry turned around, found a rock to perch on, and sat down with some effort, letting out a grunt of pain. His injuries were obviously affecting him severely.

Thaig watched him with curiosity and asked, "What are you doing?"

"I'm going to join them, Thaig. I have to. I don't know how much damage that merry band of Antennite cultists has done, or whether my men have prevailed, but I have to try to save Spire."

"You haven't answered me, Mulberry."

"You will get all the answers you seek by placing your hand on the root. You wouldn't believe me if I told you." He closed his eyes and was silent.

Thaig knew that he wouldn't get anything more out of Mulberry. He gingerly held out his fragment-encrusted hand and walked towards the root. He knew this was insanity, but it was as Mulberry said: all might very well be lost anyway. It was his curiosity, his desire to dig out the answers at any cost, that had led him down here, down to the bottom of this deep descent into madness. He wasn't about to give up before finding the final piece of the puzzle.

He rested his hand on it the root where the fragment protruded from his palm, and gripped tightly. It felt like a severe electric shock, but also like coming *home*... his senses were inflamed, his body was on fire, but he felt soothed, he was taken down, down, down...

Thaig's consciousness slipped downward into sanguine darkness. He felt like he couldn't move; *trapped!* He felt like he was wrapped in a straight-jacket, much too tight, so that his limbs lost circulation and all he knew was stinging pain. He struggled against his bonds, but to no avail.

A profound sense of abandonment came over him; a yearning for release into the black unknown that lay before him... where were the others? Why was he trapped here?

Hang on, Thaig thought - what others? This wasn't him. This was the creature. He was sharing its consciousness, or it was imparting its experiences onto him, he couldn't tell. Whatever was happening, he didn't like it. It was enough to drive somebody completely mad - somebody who didn't already have a few screws loose, that is. Somebody who hadn't had a day like Thaig had had. He understood full well why the truth was hidden; why Mulberry had warned him so severely before they proceeded.

He felt completely alien sensations; he could *feel* the creature's body as though it were his own, feel its aches and its pains, its soreness at being locked up for so long, feel all the little pinpricks of probes going up the full tubular body, all the way to the surface. He could feel the psychic cage being placed around him, boxing him in, enslaving him.

He could feel the weather - he could even exercise control over it. It was easy - like stretching out a finger. He wanted to escape, to leave, but he couldn't - he wanted to cause an earthquake of epic proportions, but the psychic hijackers stole his energy, directed it towards providing a temperate climate and rain, rain, rain...

He saw the large, ginger-haired human body of himself, Thaig, standing out there in the crowd of Antennites, screaming out for the rain to stop. He felt an incredible heave of energy, puncturing the psychic net just for an *instant*. Just enough to cease that downpour and allow the bomb fuses to light... and further this desperate plan for escape.

Thaig gasped - is that all this was, all along? From finding the root, all the way to now? All part of its fiendish fever-dreams of escaping the pacification? Maybe the creature even targeted Mine 9 because it knew Thaig was already losing it, dealing with the stimulants, with Mulberry, with Central, maybe it hunted *him* out specifically... maybe it had guided this entire set of unlikely events, through subtle psychic phenomena with the goal of bringing him here.

Thaig marvelled - he wouldn't get an answer to that, though. The creature wanted to show him something else.

The image of the black spire was projected into his mind; that part of the creature which protruded above the surface, its antenna. He saw it sticking up, stabbing the sky; he saw the pitiful city of Spire, huddled around it like inflamed infected skin around a puncture wound. He felt a deep swell of bioelectrical power, a massive potential energy which could be used to heave, to wriggle, to roar so loud that the pathetic human parasites clustered above would explode in fireworks of gore...

And before this psychic scream could leave the creature's lungs, he felt it whipped away. He felt it *stolen* away. All that energy - *taken*. He felt it being redirected by the crystalline horrors in the Chamber of the First Root, through all those little pinpricks, the probes that cut into the creature's body like scalpels, all the way along its tubular mass, all the way from the bottom to the top... to the top of the black spire.

He felt the energy being usurped and used to fire off a signal into space, amplified by the natural signal-boosting power of the creature's alien antenna.

Surprisingly, the signal was decoded into words that Thaig could understand. It said:

> *Mayday. Urgent rescue required.*
> *If you're out there, come back to us.*
> *If we're all that's left, humanity is doomed.*
> *Alien life-form found on IV.*
> *Please come back.*

———

Thaig withdrew his hand. He walked back over to Mulberry and sat down next to him, on the prone torso of an encrusted Pacifier.

Mulberry asked, "did it show you anything?"

"Yes. We're alone, aren't we."

"Absolutely alone."

"Nobody's coming for us?"

"No."

The two men sat in silence for a few moments, contemplating.

"How long have you known?"

"A select few have always known, since before the founding of Spire. Contact was lost with the offworlders not long after the colonial project on IV began, Thaig."

Thaig shook his head, clinging on to hope. "Aren't there multiple relay points? A chain of comms ships and relays going all the way back to our original settled planets?"

"There were, yes. One by one, they winked out: total signal death. We only have records of what those original colonists were told, which wasn't much. We don't know what happened to them. No mayday signals, no mention of retreat or war. They're simply *gone*."

Thaig sat back, numbed by the revelation. A black expanse enveloped him; the true loneliness of their position on Spire, on IV; the true danger that they were in, their entire existence shackled to this strange alien creature that they in turn kept shackled beneath the ground. He thought about humanity. They might be the last members of their grand spacefaring species.

"What could have happened? Alien invasion? War? Disease? What?"

"We don't know, Thaig. Wilful abandonment was touted as a possibility - maybe we were all expendable. The majority of the equipment, the workers, and the usable land all went up in smoke shortly after we landed, after all. IV is a thoroughly failed investment."

"They wouldn't!"

"You know what, Thaig, I agree with you."

"Yeah? Must be the only thing we've agreed on in our lives."

"Indeed. We can be absolutely horrible to each other sometimes, us humans, callous beyond belief. But it's highly unusual to cut off all contact to a colony like this, even a failed one. There were countless examples of failed colonies which were scooped up and deployed elsewhere. No, I fear we're alone out here. *Really* alone."

"It'll be aliens or disease or something, then," said Thaig glumly. "Extermination."

"Potentially, but we never lost heart, never lost hope... never lost hope that *someone* would be out there, even a small scouting or recon ship that could get us off IV and back to whatever remains of humanity."

"But there mightn't even be anyone else?"

"Maybe not. But we never lost hope. Our ancestors jury-rigged this creature's incredible signal-generation power and used it to shoot off mayday signals into space. And we're still doing it. That's all we've done since Spire was founded. That's what Spire *is*."

"Why can it shoot such strong signals into space?"

"Who knows? Maybe it calls out for the rest of its kind, maybe it calls out for a mate. Maybe, like us, it calls for help."

"Maybe it just screams at the futility of it all."

Mulberry smiled sadly. "Maybe."

"So, all of the mining operations here? What was the point? There was no 'quotas' to be reached before being taken off-world, was there? You've had everybody working their fingers to the bone for... *nothing*." Thaig could feel himself getting angry. The Cavern hummed with energy; the root was red.

"What is a human population without a common goal, Thaig? It tears itself apart. The instant that we reveal that we're alone, if we declare to the public that we have been abandoned, that there's no point doing *anything* until we're rescued by people that might not even exist... civil war will erupt. Spire needs a story to keep going, and that's the story: we're here to mine until we reach the necessary quota for the colonial project to end."

"And the populace should just try to ignore the strange black spire at the centre of it all, that makes them think weird thoughts? Where does that come into it?"

"I didn't say it was a perfect story. Besides, we may have been able to put together some kind of ramshackle spaceship, given enough time in the mines. It wouldn't have been capable of much, but it could have gotten a select few of us off this planet and preserved our species."

Thaig pulled out the picture of his parents and grandparents, which was crumpled into one of his many pockets. He'd brought it all the way here from his apartment. He looked at their faces; happy, despite their desperate situation on Spire. Would they have been happy if they'd known the truth? Would they have been able to forget it all and just have their wedding, just enjoy themselves for one day?

Thaig crumpled up the picture.

No.

No they wouldn't.

They lived their whole lives in pointless futility, and so did tens of thousands more over the years. And they sure as hell wouldn't have made it onto any emergency lifeboat that people like Mulberry had devised; neither would Thaig.

He stood up.

Mulberry stood up too, quicker than he did. Thaig was surprised. He looked down and saw the gun in Mulberry's hand, poking him in the ribs.

Bastard, Thaig thought; he'd taken it while Thaig had been incapacitated, while he was sharing the creature's experiences.

The cavern shook with the new level of tension and potential violence. A hundred dislocated eyes, dotted all around the cave, swivelled to watch them both.

"Stay here, Thaig," said Mulberry. "Let's both stay here. Together, we might be able to keep this thing going!"

"Not a chance, Mulberry!" Thaig shouted. "This abomination is finished! Spire is finished! Hell - *humanity is finished!*"

He really did feel like ending it all now; if *this* was what the last of humanity was reduced to, this deep, dark cave full of sad human soup, then he didn't want it to go on. Let the grand planetary monuments of past centuries and millennia be humanity's legacy unto the Universe, he thought. Let the art, the literature, the music, the history, the wars, the victories, the feats of engineering, let *those* be what humanity is remembered for...

Not *this.*

Were these Thaig's own organic thoughts, or was the creature thinking for him, spurring him on? He didn't know. He didn't care.

He head-butted Mulberry, quick as a flash. Mulberry staggered backwards and shot a bullet from his gun, which hit him in the shoulder. He didn't even feel it. Everything went quickly now, much too quickly: he was in fight-or-flight mode again. Before he knew it, he was on top of Mulberry, smashing his hand against the floor of the Cavern until he let go of the gun, and then he smashed his head against the floor too, again and again, until the light faded from his eyes, and then he brought his fists down on his face like a hammer on an anvil, again and again and again...

When Thaig calmed down, there was nothing but bloody pulp left where Mulberry's face used to be. Blood and gunk pooled into various newly-created craters in the dead man's head.

Thaig stood up and looked down at him, panting. Somehow it didn't feel as satisfying as he once thought it would; he'd fantasised about doing exactly that to Mulberry's face many times. Now that he lay dead on the floor of this gallery of freaks, Thaig barely even felt that these petty *human* squabbles mattered any more.

The cavern pulsated with the violence; cracks appeared in the walls, rocks fell from the ceiling, the root displayed a kaleidoscope of whirling bright colours. There was a loud high-pitched hissing noise that made it impossible to hear anything else. He knew that he would be left permanently deaf if he managed to survive this.

Thaig ripped off his shirt at the shoulder where he'd been shot. The bullet was lodged in his skin, halfway through the flesh. White, pearly cracks radiated from the impact site, as though a marble statue had been shot. He snorted. No going back now, he thought. He was pretty much one of these freaks already - all that separated him from these sad piles of white human slop was *time.*

He picked up Mulberry's gun from the floor, and shot the remaining bullets into the heads of those half-encrusted Pacifiers, the ones who still even had heads. To deal with the rest, he snapped off the rocky arm of one of those he'd shot. With it, he pounded every pile of pathetic sludge that he could see, in an orgy of brutal freak-extermination that saw every misplaced eye in the Cavern of the First Root wink out.

The creature roared and screamed; a ringing filled the air that was akin to a choir singing, Thaig's entire being fizzed and popped as though his blood were carbonated, and he felt *free, free, joyously free!*

He looked and laughed, sweaty and wild-eyed, as the paralysed root wriggled free, and moved like the tentacle of an octopus freed from decades of imprisonment. He saw it slip back out of the back of the Cavern through a hole, impossibly quick, and the earth shook beneath and around him with the unmistakable ferocity of a hopelessly severe earthquake.

He dropped to his knees and screamed, waiting for the cavern to collapse upon him. Just before it did so, the root whipped back through the hole, wrapped around his waist, and dragged him out.

Thaig, the creature's favourite disciple, the architect of its escape, was going with it.

Thaig soared, up through the cavern beneath the Central part of Spire, past the murderous Antennite cultists and the beleaguered security staff, up through the ceiling, up into the sky... he couldn't know whether he saw with his own eyes, or whether he simply experienced what the creature experienced.

He saw the cataclysm beneath him radiating outward, a vast shockwave. He watched entire districts of Spire lifted up like the roots beneath an upturned tree. Entire streets and blocks were thrown outward and landed upon other streets and blocks further out. The land was torn up and folded, and an almighty gash was all that was left of the city once known as Spire.

He felt an ecstatic joy; it radiated out from the creature with such force that all the hapless residents of Spire felt it too; they died in rapturous glee, laughing and screaming at the sky, at the bright and beautiful alien shape that they saw ascending to the heavens. They waved their limbs in crazed unison with the wriggling roots of the creature, and then they were gone.

He watched the remains of the ruined planet once known as IV erupt in a fiery inferno, and then his vision turned to the stars.

He wasn't sure when he died, exactly; he couldn't pinpoint the exact moment. Maybe he hit his head on the way out of the Cavern of the First Root; maybe he was pounded to pulp when the creature burst through the city; maybe he disintegrated in the harsh atmospheres above IV.

It didn't matter. A part of him lived on, merged within that fantastic creature's consciousness; his eternal heavenly reward, bestowed upon him by the strange and glorious alien that he had helped to set free. Whether or not any more humans remained in the Universe was no longer of any concern to him. He had left humanity behind.

. . .

That portion of Thaig's psyche rode on into space, forever stitched to the creature's unfathomable consciousness, accompanying it on its unfathomable stellar errands. Thaig would live forever, clinging on for dear life, on a rapturous psychic joyride into the twinkling beyond.

Printed in Great Britain
by Amazon